ATOM

ATOM

By

Lennon Nersesian

iUniverse, Inc.

New York   Bloomington

Atom

iUniverse books may be ordered through booksellers or by contacting:

*iUniverse
1663 Liberty Drive
Bloomington, IN 47403
www.iuniverse.com
1-800-Authors (1-800-288-4677)*

*ISBN: 9781440143571 (pbk)
ISBN: 9781440143564 (ebk)*

Printed in the United States of America

iUniverse rev. date: 5/15/2009

To all who have made up my memory burners.

In memory of Atom

"When broken down to our most basic component, we are Atom."

CHAPTER ONE

The spaces between the lines began to blur as he headed down another highway, assured that he would get to where he was going because he had no destination in mind. Switching on his mental cloaking device, insulated from the trappings of sound, people, and weather, his controlled environment provided the necessary recipe for self-evaluation and inventory. His hands alternated between gripping the steering wheel to slapping the sides of his face in an attempt to remain alert enough to complete his analysis. His consignment stock was overdue and he was delinquent in payment, and even though he knew he didn't have a solution to his dilemma, he was sure the answer lay ahead...as it usually did.

Nothing looked familiar, but all seemed the same. He was tired, though not just physically. His ongoing bout with erectile dysfunction and his chronic heart condition paled in comparison to his depression and anger. Justifying his failed existence by blaming the actions of others was a full-time job. Even though his job was dependent on his ability to communicate and influence people's decisions, it was people he could not stand.

He parked in a spot where the meter still had time left, interestingly at a storefront marked PALM READING *Guaranteed*. Curious, sick, and tired, with no strategy or plan, desperate for an answer, or at least a suggestion, he entered.

* * * * *

She knew Norman like the back of his hand. Gloria was the self-proclaimed best palm reader in the East Village, analyzing each one of her clients with grace and accuracy. She had the touch of a masseuse and the foresight of a visionary, reading deeper into one's lines than any other. Unlike the many impostors, Gloria truly believed that peoples' hands were the blueprint to their past and the passport to their future.

"Palm reading is so natural, we all do it," Gloria would pitch to her customers. "It's no coincidence that when we first meet others, we shake their hands to get a sense of their character. It's the purest, most elementary form of palm reading we have."

Gloria never had formal training. She didn't require the nonsensical mystical decorations and wizardry ornaments adorning her place of business to prove her reading skills and attract customers.

"Leave that nonsense to the psychics and the doctors," she often said.

Gloria never understood why doctors would hang

their diplomas in the examination rooms. If these self-aggrandizing glorified medicine men felt they still needed to sell themselves to their patients by the time they had their pants around their ankles, then they must not be too confident in themselves or their diagnoses.

"A doctor's diploma is the crystal ball and the tarot cards of their profession," Gloria believed. "Nothing more than plastic testimonies for their experiences yet to be realized."

It was this arrogant attitude that made her the best. Gloria believed she provided a priceless service, much more valuable than any white coat could ever accord, allowing her patients to understand their unique world and carry it around with them in the palms of their hands for the rest of their lives.

"I give my patients the power to heal themselves," Gloria professed, taking another stab at the medical community.

However, in all of her years of palm reading, she had never come across hands like Norman's.

Of course, Gloria was able to discern many of Norman's attributes without studying his palms, a tactic she practiced with all of her clients. The first thing she noticed was Norman's grizzly beard. How could she not? It concealed most of his face like a homegrown Halloween costume of a Civil War foot soldier. Gloria saw those who wore beards as a way of keeping others from identifying the real people behind them; the more facial hair, the more there was to hide. Norman was ensconced.

Norman's eyes also appeared to be stuck in a permanent squint position, which Gloria perceived as another untrustworthy trait. What he was hiding beyond the concealed white expanse surrounding the universe in his pupils Gloria hoped to excavate from the trenches of his hands. Gloria considered the eyes as the second best judge of a person's character, only when the curtains are pulled all the way up. The hands, on the other hand, can't prevaricate or be obscured.

Gloria also gleaned that the subject was not a local. His complete lack of familiarity and respect for Gloria's reputation was evident. This surprised Gloria. In her little world, there wasn't a hand that didn't know her. This was the first time she wished her credentials were on the wall.

"Twenty-five dollars for fifteen minutes."

"Twenty-five dollars? Does that include a manicure?"

"Obviously, you haven't heard of me. No, that's extra. If you didn't notice when you walked in, my palm reading is guaranteed."

"Do I get a discount if I mention I'm staying at the Sunnyside Inn?" Norman negotiated, as he reached for his wallet.

"Do you want me to validate your parking, too?"

Norman grunted as he placed $25 on the table.

"Show me your hands."

Norman slowly exposed his hands from his pants pockets, another partition separating him from his secrets. He rested his hands on his knees and waited for subsequent instructions. Norman had nowhere to be and was taking his time.

In the 25 years Gloria had been practicing palm reading, she noticed that there were basically three different types of people who sought her services. The most common visitors were the non-believers, those who didn't mind wasting everyone's time for a cheap thrill and a story to tell. Gloria would put a little scare into these adolescent troublemakers with melodramatic exaggerations of the shortcomings in the length of their lifeline. Norman did not fall into this category. His deafening silence and his serious stare signified that this was no joking matter.

The second group of people in need of evaluation was those looking for a little reassurance. In these cases, Gloria would provide the necessary dose of self-confidence, focusing on the positives of their wealth and love line. Again, Norman was not a fit. His cool demeanor conveyed a hint of arrogance and fortitude in his conviction, whether justified or not, which she surmised needed no reassurance.

The last group in need of a hand read was those in search of a direction or a path toward a better life. Usually, a map could be found by following the long and broken fate or travel line. First impression of Norman yielded that of a lost middle-aged man destined for a journey to find the soul behind the beard. In Gloria's opinion, Norman was the poster child for the third group.

"Don't be shy, you're in good hands."

Norman reluctantly placed his hands on the table, palms down, and waited for Gloria to guide them over with her long red fingernails.

Gloria wasn't drawn to the sight of his unusually busy palms, which under normal circumstances would have kept her occupied for hours. Norman's lines were as deep and cavernous as the surface of the moon and as complicated as the overlapping Los Angeles highways. If reading the average customer's palms were like translating a standard-length novella, then interpreting Norman's would be like struggling through *War and Peace;* Gloria anticipated his lines would be riddled with just as much human drama and heartache.

None of that mattered at the moment.

What immediately caught Gloria's eye was Norman's unsuccessful attempt to re-author the story in his lines or add one final chapter. Gloria did not need her 25 years of experience to interpret the two freshly made scars running across the length of both his wrists.

"Have an accident?" Gloria asked nervously, knowing that wasn't the case.

"I fell," Norman responded robotically. "Just tell me what my hands say," he said through heavy inhales, disrupting an otherwise emotionless exterior. "Go ahead. Tell me that I don't control my own destiny."

"Everyone controls their own destiny, Mr. Tate," Gloria shot back, as she continued to study the self-inflicted cuts on Norman's wrists. "It's what you do when destiny comes knocking on your door. That's what defines you."

Norman volleyed a cold heavy stare back across the table. Sensing the tension, Gloria considered she treat Norman like a non-believer and send him on his way before there was any trouble. She began following his lines, slowly, almost as if reading Braille for the first time. Normally, Gloria started her read with the lifeline before commencing further east to the head and heart line; however, Norman's hand directed her south.

Gloria was reading a tragedy. The main character was a sad and lonely nomad who learned to love nobody but himself. Norman was definitely in need of some guidance. Gloria hoped to point him in the right direction.

"There seems to be a lot of breaks in your lifeline," Gloria pointed out. "Do you feel like your life is unraveling?" She tried to stop herself from finishing the question because she feared Norman's response would be less than cooperative.

It was no secret that Norman's life must have been spiraling out of control. He tattooed his troubles on his wrists and then visited a palm reader. It was a cry for help. The last thing Norman needed to hear was a stranger parade the obvious around like it was a revelation. Gloria needed to be extra careful, which was why she didn't give him time to answer and immediately transitioned into another discovery.

"Do you see how the end of your lifeline splits? You are at a crossroads in your life, and you will be forced to choose a path to your future."

Gloria felt Norman's hands moistening.

What surprised this seasoned palm reader the most about the session was the depth and wavy nature of Norman's fate line, signifying how little control he actually had over his life. There was an outside force telling him which way to turn. Gloria didn't think it would be wise to inform him of this fact, not after her supposedly poignant speech earlier about Norman's supposed self-determination.

"There is a definite relationship between your lifeline and fate line. It suggests a low depressive period around the age of sixteen, and the discoloration indicates problems that show interference with your family. I have rarely seen this, but it illustrates a strong dichotomy. On one hand, you have a strong loyalty to your family, and on the other, you seem to be running from their memory."

The muscles in Norman's hands tightened.

"Tell me about your past," Gloria requested, as her fingers tried to escape a dead-end cul-de-sac off Norman's unusually faint heart line.

Gloria was treading a fine line between palm reading and psychiatry.

"What are you, a psychiatrist or a palm reader? You tell me. You seem to have me all figured out already."

Gloria, taken aback by his sudden defense, almost removed her fingers from Norman's hands, which in the palm reading world was a disrespectful sign of giving up on the client's read. Norman, who wasn't even privy to the palm reader's code, grabbed Gloria's fingers with a tight suffocating grip and pulled her in over the table so she couldn't escape. He squeezed her moneymakers until the blood evaded the stranglehold causing her fingers to become numb. Norman's eyes opened wide for the first time as he glared at Gloria. As the curtain rose on the show, Gloria was certain it was no love story. "If you only want to hear what you want to hear," Gloria said, wincing from the pain in her hands, "…then why are you here?"

"You're all the same."

Norman threw Gloria's hands back in her face. No longer calm, cool, and collected as if he had all the time in the world, Norman took his insolent palms and stormed out the door. "They're all the same," Norman said.

Gloria's world was shaken. For the first time, she felt the unfamiliar feeling of failure, possibly reopening the wounds on Norman's wrist for him to dig a little deeper in search of answers.

Maybe he would have been better off seeing a doctor, she wondered. *Maybe the MD would have found something more substantial with Norman's pants around his ankles.*

She convinced herself of her omnipotence, and could not accept defeat. As Gloria rubbed her burning hands and contemplated her legacy, she vowed to prove her diagnosis correct. Her prescription would not be denied. A life depended on it. After failing to get through to a patient for the first time, Gloria had some digging to do herself, and Norman provided her with the shovel.

Gloria's own neglected hands could not have prepared her for their meeting. Her introduction to Norman was not all that unusual.

CHAPTER TWO

Jason Strykowski had a problem. He was the keynote member of an endangered species. If you needed to locate Jason, he could be found swinging from the highest limb on his family tree. However, the Strykowski tree, which had survived 13 generations, was rapidly decaying without Jason's seed.

The proud Strykowski name outlived six wars, three plagues, two natural disasters, and one depression, but it may have met its match with one pivotal insider's inadequacy at building relationships and spawning offspring.

If it were up to Jason, he would prefer to go to the grave with his family name - be the last to carry the Strykowski torch across the finish line - but the budding branches just below Jason's canopy were pressuring him into a life of sustenance and procreation. Jason's father constantly reminded him of the contributions his great-grandfather made to help establish Denmark as a modern welfare state. His uncle was not subtle in his message when lecturing Jason on his ancestor's heroic relocation to the United States to escape German occupation during World War II. Even his mother, who wasn't even blessed with Strykowski blood, ominously warned Jason of the consequences for retiring a historic name full of tradition.

"Did you know that you have royal blood in you?" his mother would say on more than one occasion. Jason was unsure to the validity of her statement, but would never dispute her suspicious allegations and dubious motives. "You would be doing the world a major disservice if you didn't settle down."

Jason began to wonder why he was an only child if his family was so preoccupied about preserving the family name. *They deserve some of the blame, too*, he concluded. His father's two brothers each gave it two unsuccessful attempts, accounting for Jason's four female cousins. Why couldn't Jason's parents increase the odds with a second try? Instead, they were satisfied with their firstborn and were fully confident with putting all their potential future grandsons into one extremely awkward basket. Over 300 years of history unfairly rested on the last fertile male Strykowski's shoulders and he wasn't interested in the challenge.

Even though he valued his independence, Jason was not against becoming a father to either a boy or girl, if the right situation presented itself. He would be an active parent, probably coach Little League, or even become president of the PTA. What he would never do is pressure his children to conceive for the sake of some dead people with the same last name. To offset his parents' indoctrination, he would tell his children that they didn't live for the needs of others.

Jason held firmly to the idea that if the Strykowski name died off it could only be of natural causes. Jason's mother would rebut by noting there was nothing natural about the way his only son was living his life. According to Mrs. Strykowski, people were not meant to die alone, and that was exactly what would happen to Jason if he didn't make more of an effort to meet someone to spend the rest of his days with. She used all of the guilt a mother could fabricate to will her son out of his social malaise.

In the end, she didn't care about his happiness. None of his family did. He had a much more important pursuit. Happiness could be a possible secondary effect.

"You don't even have to get married," his desperate mother would tell him, expressing how much she actually cared about his own wishes. A comment like that hurt Jason the most, even more so than when his uncle slipped him the number of a reputable stripper and a package of defective condoms, both of which he never used. "You're killing your father, you know."

Jason went 45 years without a serious relationship. It would be easy to blame his career as a legal counsel for not having any personal dating time, but even he would have to admit that his insecurity around women played a small role in his lonely situation. He never felt comfortable in the presence of the opposite sex. He tried too hard to impress and would come away looking desperate. He became accustomed to riding the third wheel at any of the social gatherings he attended and slowly rode that wheel into a comfortable state of apathy as the rest of his friends found love and raised children on top of their respective family trees like happy little monkeys.

Jason dreamed of taking the hedge clipper to the lower branches not supporting his isolated view up top on his own family tree. The Strykowski insecurity gene should have surrendered to Darwin's survival of the fittest theory long ago, but it was Jason's insecurity that turned his ancestors over in their graves. Jason's great-great-great grandfather must have thought he was such a loser.

As Jason navigated through middle age by himself, he helplessly watched his father deteriorate from an inoperable brain tumor, which Mrs. Strykowski believed Jason inspired. Jason reluctantly decided to heed his dying father's last wishes to save the family tree from being uprooted and go on a quest to find the woman who would bear the future of the Strykowski name.

Sounds romantic, Jason joked. He presumed that if he took the romance out of the equation and turned the dating game into a sterile contest, then maybe he could find success developing relationships with women other than his four cousins. *Maybe my mother was right about the romance being a consequence of the putative higher goal,* he continued to wonder. Jason Strykowski's investigation began on his lunch break at the local elementary school where he participated in a speed dating exercise, hoping to test out his new theory and approach.

All of the pathetic single men donned nametags and sat at third grade school desks waiting to be introduced to eight different women during the course of the event. The men had three minutes to get to know each of the female participants. When the three minutes elapsed, the chairman blew a whistle and the girls rotated around the room until everyone had a chance to meet. Cupcakes and apple juice were served free of charge after the formal proceedings. Jason felt very optimistic with his chances, not because he was the only one who did not display *pathetic* on his nametag like all the others, but because he was the only one not seeking any love. All he wanted was a breeding partner to remove his name from the endangered species list. None of those doting sentiments that create and destroy relationships could ever get in the way of his goal. Nevertheless, Jason and his insecurity gene never needed the full three minutes to end any of his eight dates that day. It must have been something he said because he implemented the perfect strategy for what he deemed to be a failsafe plan. A typical transcript for one of Jason's eight dates would have been covered with judgmental red ink marks if it ever got into the hands of a relationship therapist.

The transcript would have read as follows:

Date #4:   What do you do for a living?
  Jason: I have royalty in my blood.
Date #4:   Excuse me?
  Jason: Have you ever seen *The Twilight Zone?*
Date #4:   Yes, why?
  Jason: My grandfather was the lead actor in Episode Four of Season 5.
Date #4:   Sounds like you have a wonderful family.
  Jason: Would you like to become a member?
Date #4:   A member of what?
  Jason: I can give you the password to enter the Strykowski tree house.

Date #4:   Who do you think you are?
   Jason: I'm in a bit of a pickle. Maybe you can help.

There was nothing subtle about Jason's approach. He must have acquired that trait from his uncle. Including all of the awkward pauses, the one-sided conversation lasted about 55 seconds. Jason didn't even get to explain his situation to any of the eight women, as if they would understand. He may have been better off playing the insecure and desperate loser he spent 45 years rehearsing to become. If his nametag didn't read *pathetic*, then he was certainly misleading his dates. The chairman's whistle could not have sounded quick enough.

Jason didn't stay for refreshments. He was more determined than ever. Just because he failed at speed dating didn't mean he was going to forfeit the mission. He would make some adjustments to his strategy, but he was set on the overall plan. There had to be someone out there willing to enter a loveless relationship to save the Strykowski family tree.

CHAPTER THREE

What is happening in his head? Rebecca wondered, hopefully for the last time. She woke up this morning on a mission to justify her last seven years.

His name was Atom, pronounced like God's first attempt at man, but spelled like a chemist's scientific rebuttal. Atom was once a chemist, but wasn't pressured into the profession by his name. He willingly followed his father's leap into the highest energy levels, studying quantum chemistry at MIT, later notoriously recognized for his radical contributions in the field of reactive molecular collisions and the density-functional theory. His controversial findings, which precluded him from ever teaching at the university, could be found in *The International Journal of Quantum Chemistry,* a publication his father failed several times to permeate.

It is the only lasting record of Atom's former self.

If you notified Atom of his reputation, he wouldn't believe you. He might smile and nod his head, but that would be the extent to his recognition, no matter how many times you reminded him of his professional discoveries. Rebecca, Atom's personal nurse at the South Cove Manor Nursing Home, had spent several years trying to get him to acknowledge anything from his past, to no avail.

Atom suffered from Alzheimer's disease. Simply learning this fact about him was already more than he would ever know about himself. Files once stored in his long-term memory bank vanished as if they were his ninth grade locker combination. Names of family and friends escaped his mind forever, leaving only an entity present in the moment with no burdens, no expectations. Atom had become ionized, a nucleus without any electrons. Despite Atom's degenerative shortcomings, Rebecca tested his cognitive abilities daily, demanding a recollection, any recollection, not only for his health, which she safeguarded as if it were her own, but also for her sanity.

Rebecca refused to submit to the notion that memories needed to be returned as if they were overdue borrowed library books. She was determined to have Atom remember his past. It scared her to accept that memories could be time sensitive, eradicating moments, and erasing identity. If she could succeed in bringing Atom's memories back home, she knew she would never lose her way.

Who are we if we can't remember who we were? Rebecca asked herself.

Every morning at exactly 11:30, Rebecca would

visit Atom, equipped with tea for two. She hoped this regular routine would condition Atom's fleeting memory into expecting her visit. Not once in the seven years of her habitual exercise did Atom show any signs of recollection.

It was over tea where Rebecca would share with Atom all of her thoughts. If Atom had the power of retention, then he would be an expert in Rebecca's life, possibly even a much-needed father figure carrying the advice she was so desperately searching for in her own pursuit. It was a liberating feeling for Rebecca, having somebody to finally share her life with; however, she cried herself to sleep at night knowing that Atom's brain didn't have the compatible adhesive for her words to stick.

She wept for Atom. She wept for herself.

"How was your night?" Rebecca asked while steeping Atom's tea, hoping that this would be the day he broke out of his mental anguish and described in full detail what an Alzheimer's patient dreamt about so she wouldn't have to follow through with her underdeveloped plan. She fantasized that all of his memories emerged from their daytime hiding place to gently rock Atom into a well-deserved peaceful sleep. Realistically, Rebecca guessed that the only things he saw when he closed his eyes were the colorful, oversaturated residual images from the bright lights in the room, fading as quickly as his memory of them.

"Do you remember my name?"

"Alex," Atom grunted.

Rebecca lowered her head and sighed. "What's your name?"

Atom did not respond. He was never good with

names, especially his own, which seemed to change from day to day. Memory to memory, He took his tea and stared out the window smiling. If any passersby on the street happened to catch a glimpse of him gazing outside, they would have seen an old man who appeared extremely content with himself in the moment. They would not have known about his hellish condition as Rebecca did. Understanding Atom was like trying to read one of his chemistry textbooks with no index. Rebecca struggled through more pages than anybody else did, but came away with no information or balanced formulas.

Except for what was documented in *The IJQC,* which was too technical for Rebecca's limited understanding of Chemistry 101, her only other knowledge of Atom's past came from what she could piece together during teatime. The lines on his face seemed more plentiful than the hair on his head. He liked watching black & white movies, his favorite being *Casablanca.* The staff played the movie on a constant loop for Atom. He would watch it four or five times in a row, enjoying each screening as if he were seeing it for the first time. He loved pea soup and disliked grilled cheese sandwiches. He spoke in non-sequiturs, borrowing phrases from TV shows and other patients and nurses at the home.

That was all Rebecca could gather about Atom. She didn't have much help though. In the seven years she had been nursing him, not one person visited. No friends or family checked up on him. Efforts to locate his sister were futile. No fellow chemists came to debate his noteworthy theories on electromagnetism and carbon bonding. It saddened Rebecca, probably because she could relate to the solitude.

"My mother used to make tea for me every Sunday when I was a little girl," Rebecca told Atom, as he continued to stare out the window, straight at an abutting brick building. "We would drink them in these little pink plastic cups..."

"Xavior fermented Chinese chocolate moose cake into a magnificent pony and jumped over the moon three times!" Atom shouted out the window.

Frustrated again, Rebecca cried.

Seven years worth of dedication, commitment, and energy polluted tears of hope and design into desperation. Teatime wasn't working, and for her own selfish sake, she needed to attempt a more aggressive treatment with Atom's disease. After all, they suffered from the same affliction. The only difference was Atom was in his sixties and didn't have a past to look back on whereas Rebecca was in her early thirties and didn't have a future to look forward to. The roles should have been reversed.

There wasn't much more time to solve the medical mystery. It wouldn't be long before Atom reached Alzheimer's fatal third stage, at which point his body would descend the same degenerative path as his brain. Rebecca wiped the tears sliding down her cheeks and approached Atom with a loosely designed plan with an unpredictable consequence.

"We're going to hunt down your memories," she promised to Atom's Alzheimer's, understanding that it wouldn't hold her to any false promises made.

"One thousand sheep and ten million flamingos," he responded.

Rebecca believed that whatever he just said was approval for what she was about to do. She grabbed hold of Atom's wheelchair and weighed her options. Even if she could get past the nurses in the hallway, the receptionist would definitely stop her before they could escape out the front entrance. The fire escape by the men's bathroom was set to an alarm, and unless she wanted to draw more attention to herself with flashing lights, that door was out of the question, too.

There was only one other alternative, and upon that realization, her prevailing concern shifted from where to how. Rebecca wheeled Atom aside and gently lifted the window, all the while wondering how she was going to convince him to climb out.

CHAPTER FOUR

"I keep my closet door open all day so that my untimely wall clock can face all of its inadequacies in the reflection of my mirror," the hotel light fixture said to the know-it-all TV guide. The carpet prepared a carefully planned, reasonable argument. Sideways glasses contemplated the meaning of life, but couldn't philosophize or look past the present. "We're all furniture," summarized the rocking chair.

Norman was hearing voices again. This time they were making sense. The razor blades were not within reach.

Norman's hands were burning as he stood in front of the bathroom mirror of room 235 at the Sunnyside Inn. He blamed Gloria. She must have placed a hex on his palms. That was Norman's only conceivable explanation. He remembered learning about palm readers who laced their fingertips with toxic chemicals to infect their clients.

Norman would not put a cheap stunt like that past Gloria. Although he was cynical and distrustful with just about everybody he met, Norman felt the most cynical and the most distrustful toward Gloria, the master palm reader, maybe because she knew too much.

Not once was Norman satisfied with a fortuneteller's judgments. They always seemed to concoct vague generalizations about a future from oversimplified projections. Norman denied Gloria's reading, and was convinced it could have applied to anybody with two open hands and one closed mind. What bothered Norman the most was that whenever these existential crooks could not find anything positive to forecast, they delved into the back roads of his past, despite unambiguous instructions not to make the backward trek.

Norman made a promise that Gloria's reading would be his last; whether or not he received the answers he was looking for. It became very apparent early on in the session that she had none of the solutions. He called it quits for good only five minutes into Gloria's no-money-back charade. However, anybody who was unlucky enough to meet Norman would know he'd return to a similar establishment in another town for another reading, if only for the slightest of human contact.

Despite the expert's allegations, Norman believed he had just the right amount of human contact to keep a man sane. His job demanded he interact with others on a daily basis. He probably spoke to more strangers in one day than the average person did in a lifetime. *Try selling vacuums door to door without relating to others*, Norman defended.

Listening to Norman try to sell you something was

like getting a root canal from a dentist with bad teeth or a haircut from a bald barber. It was hard to believe he could ever deliver the goods based on first impressions. The elementary tips and guidelines taught in Sales 101 was a necessary practice for every successful door-to-door industry professional except for Norman. He was rewriting the rulebook.

To be fair, he was at an obvious disadvantage. The first rule in developing a concrete sales pitch is to be honest and friendly with potential customers, which was impossible for Norman to apply. His behavior with Gloria during the short-lived palm reading session was no fluke and not exclusive to his sorry excuse for a personal life. Arrogance and inhospitableness were also the foundations that grounded his warped sales technique.

While most of his colleagues would be sociable in their pitch, slowly working to bring down the customer's resistance level by earning their trust with small talk and relatable stories before closing the deal, Norman wasted no time going in for the kill, attacking the customer's shield with intimidating price quotes and non-negotiable offers. Norman confused his customers' resistance level for their tolerance level, and more often than not, walked away without a sale.

The second most important rule for any salesman is to believe in the product you are representing. Norman had no use for the bagless Power Hum Vac 3500X with the odor shield and the self-propelled rotating brush roll. Until they invented a vacuum that could clean the cobwebs in the hard to reach places of a person's soul, only then would Norman find an application for the product he was selling.

Norman felt most uncomfortable when he had to demonstrate the vacuum's powerful capabilities in strangers' homes. He was no longer a salesman at that point. He begrudgingly accepted the role as an unpaid housekeeper while the homeowner pretended to be interested in the sale for a free cleaning. Nothing bothered Norman more than being played a fool. He would make sure to vacuum every square inch of the carpet, including under the couch and in-between the radiator vents until the homeowner appeared more than satisfied with the cleaning. After the presentation, he would display all of the dust that the Power Hum Vac 3500X collected from the carpet. If still unable to close, Norman would politely thank them for their time and return the dust from whence it came.

Norman took great pleasure in dumping the dust full of memories back onto the carpet. The look on their faces almost made the entire experience worth his maid service.

Even if Norman did not sell any vacuums, he always left his mark, but not the kind of mark stressed in the third and final rule for becoming a successful salesman: you must be able to sell yourself as if you were the product. Some experts deem this to be the most important rule of all.

Norman never bothered putting his defective self on the market to help sell a vacuum cleaner. He must have realized that when you suck more than the product you are selling, it would be pretty hard to peddle yourself to the customers. Besides, Norman felt like he had been bought and sold long ago, and would be doing the consumers a favor by not including himself as a special offer in the sale.

After a serious analysis, the experts and Norman were both right. The tragic door-to-door vacuum salesman may have had the appropriate amount of human contact to satisfy his needs; however, the contact he made could have well as been with a 20-foot pole. Norman made a decision. This was to be his last day as a vacuum salesman.

None of the aforementioned tricks of the trade would have helped Norman survive his final road trip with the Power Hum Vac 3500X, his only companion other than the friend he saw just about every morning for 20 minutes while trimming his beard and brushing his teeth. Norman and his two compatriots were about to embark on another one of his scheduled ego trips, where failing to sell vacuum cleaners was a misfortunate pit stop to an endless journey out of his own suffocating vacuum he called his life. The lonely trio was in for a surprise that none of the sales experts could have prepared him for.

It began with a soft knock on his hotel room door.

"Who is it?" Norman asked, annoyed to have been interrupted while preparing for work. He wanted to be on the road by nine so he was finished by lunchtime.

"Front desk. I have a package for you."

Norman wasn't expecting a package. Nobody even knew of his whereabouts. He closed his suitcase, which was packed tight with all of his belongings - poor reminders of the past - and left it on the bed as he suspiciously approached the door.

"Just a minute," Norman muttered, trying to buy time as he performed a perfunctory background check through the peephole. The world looked eerily similar to Norman through the peephole as it did for him all the time. The fish-eyed figure was the clerk from the front desk holding a small package, confirming his identity.

Norman unchained the door and received ownership of the package from the clerk without any transfer of dialogue, gesture, or gratuity.

It was a small package wrapped in brown Kraft paper and on it was handwritten: TO NORMAN TATE with a return address that read: "YOUR LAST HOPE."

Is this a sick joke? Norman asked himself. He only had two friends. Vacuum cleaners weren't known for being particularly giving and Norman's reflection never did anything nice for him, let alone for others. *There had to be a mistake,* Norman continued to assess.

There was only one way to find out.

Norman ripped open the box. He pulled out a handwritten note and a GPS device for the car. He unfolded the note and read the letter aloud.

Here's to helping you find a little direction in your life. Remember, you are at a crossroads. Make sure to follow the correct path to your future.

Your last hope,
Gloria

The tag line on the GPS read: *The perfect companion for when you don't know where you're going!*

"Well, this is a first. Maybe I underestimated her ability," Norman wondered.

Norman grabbed his suitcase and exited the hotel room. He could see his friend, the Power Hum Vac 3500X, sleeping in the backseat of his car. Norman was excited to introduce him to his new friend. The GPS called shotgun.

CHAPTER FIVE

They had successfully escaped through the window at the South Cove Manor Nursing Home, unnoticed by any of the other nurses or security guards. Rebecca knew it would only be a matter of time when someone came to check on Atom, only to find two cups of lukewarm tea and an open window letting in the breeze. The concerned party would then search all over the estate for his personal nurse. Rebecca hoped to be three counties away by the time they realized her car was missing from the employee lot.

Rebecca was doing 90. Not once during the 150,000 miles she logged on the non-distinctive pale green midsize Camry with brown trim had she driven so fast. She was never a criminal on the run before. She was surprised she could excite her 10-year-old vehicle to such impressive heights on the speedometer. Atom sat in the passenger's seat seeming to enjoy every moment of high speed, not preoccupied with the consequences of their illegal actions. He left that responsibility to the nervous kidnapper cursed with the debilitating condition of thought.

They know my car and have a record of my plates, Rebecca feared. Maybe she didn't think this plan through as well as she thought she did.

Rebecca needed to get her car off the road. Fast. Unfortunately, there was only one person in her vicinity who could help her continue with her mission unmarked. She would have avoided the following encounter if there were other options.

There were no other options.

Walter Benson lived two exits away. At the current authority-challenging pace, she'd be at his doorstep in seven minutes. Rebecca vowed never to see her ex-boyfriend again, but now she was driving 25 miles over the speed limit for his help, which she feared would come at a devastating price.

If Atom were able to remember any of Rebecca's teatime confessions, he would have done everything in his power to convince her not to seek Walter's assistance; reminding her of all the times he cheated and abused the relationship. He was probably home screwing some floozy waitress, which wouldn't be unlike the last confrontation Rebecca had with Walter. It didn't matter anymore though.

The other nurses at the home were correct in their assumptions that Rebecca would ultimately run back to Walter. Rebecca overheard her co-workers gossiping behind her back often. The only solace she had was the belief in her convictions.

Even with all of the rumors swirling around about Rebecca at the nursing home, none of the chatty nurses would have predicted she'd ever abduct a patient. She didn't seem like the type. Suicide maybe, never a kidnapping. Rebecca was too timid and submissive to ever display the upper hand in any relationship, especially the kidnapper-kidnapee association, which required a most dominating presence for the bond to exist. Rebecca showed no signs of dominance, even over Atom.

Maybe they'll think we were both kidnapped, Rebecca hoped, despite understanding that it wouldn't make a difference. They'd still look for her car.

"What am I thinking?" Rebecca asked herself, second-guessing the plan for the first time. It was too late. There was no turning back now, even though the pioneer destination appeared more formidable than her starting point at the home.

With one exit to go before her impromptu date with Walter, Rebecca reminisced, using Atom as an Etch-A-Sketch to temporarily record her emotions.

"Every summer morning when my brother and I were kids, we'd sit out on the dock by the lake at our house up in Maine and dip our feet in the water until we were called in for lunch," Rebecca explained while lost at sea on the rolling waves in her eyes. "Our feet looked like shriveled little balls by the time we took them out of the water. You should have seen us try to run back to the house."

Rebecca laughed joyfully, a nice respite, if only for a moment.

"My men are rounding up twice the number of usual

suspects," Atom replied, his memory bank shaken clean of Rebecca's sketch of the past.

The exit had arrived. Rebecca could have continued soaking her feet in the memory of her childhood lake, but the cold hard reality beckoned her back into the gravity of the moment. Her feet were already numb anyway.

Rebecca slowed down to 50 on the side roads. On a normal day, she would have been worried about cops hiding out in speed traps while only driving 10 miles per hour over the posted speed limits, but priorities weren't a constant in the experiment of life. Her mind was elsewhere. Besides, Rebecca didn't think she was driving fast enough. She was only trying to keep up with her world, which was spinning out of control at a million miles per hour.

As the pale green midsize Camry with brown trim rocketed past Sullivan Street, Rebecca had to hurdle a series of yellow school zone speed bumps while maintaining her MacGyver speed. Atom bounced up and down in his seat, enjoying the ride like a child at an amusement park.

Walter's house was in sight. It lured Rebecca in like a paperclip to a magnet. If Rebecca were a paperclip, she would have had her things together. Rather, she was all over the place. Rebecca could not offset the sudden influx of horrible memories, originally spawned inside Walter's house as terrifying experiences, from making their way back into her conscience. Dipping her eight-year-old toes in the lake of her imagination wouldn't help her counteract the panic.

Pulling into Walter's driveway felt like a punch to the gut. All of her breath cowardly escaped to safety as she stared down the entrance. The front door was dirt gray, representing the color of the inhabitant within. She didn't want to knock on the door because she anticipated its touch would be as cold as death.

"I'll be right back," she explained to Atom. "Don't move, understand?"

He wasn't going anywhere. He was happy right where he was.

Other than the gray door, Walter's abode did not emit an evil odor. Returning after a three-year absence, Rebecca was expecting the Amityville Horror house. That was how she had it burned into her memory. The rose bushes abutting against the garage were inviting. The bedroom windows weren't keeping any secrets, as if there was nothing for them to hide from the outside world. Even the rustic railing summoned visitors to the door with promises of support up the stoop.

Walter's house was a typical middle-class ranch with moderate upkeep. A perfect disguise. The ill-prepared traveler would have mistaken it for an engaging habitat. Rebecca hiked through Walter's wilderness in the past and she was no better equipped to defend herself from the animals lurching inside than when she was previously attacked.

As Rebecca approached, her determination was breached. Exiting Walter's house was what appeared to be another hiker, equipped with a device to clear his way. It was a door-to-door vacuum salesman, and from the looks of him, no sale had been made. The two hikers passed each other, made eye contact, but each unable to acknowledge the other's existence. Atom watched from the car.

"I'm sorry. I was too young to comprehend the consequences, but it doesn't absolve my actions," Atom confessed in the car's cone of silence. He was his only audience. "I shouldn't have retaliated."

Rebecca rang the doorbell and waited. She expected to find an ambulance of gossipy nurses tearing down the street, lights blazing and sirens blaring. They'd take her away, not in handcuffs, but on a gurney in restraints.

She heard footsteps. Walter was home and en route to the door. As he approached, his footsteps were getting louder to keep up with Rebecca's heartbeat.

The gray front door swung open.

"Well, well, if it isn't Becca," Walter snorted, holding out his hand in greeting, which looked more like an elephant's foot than a hand. "What brings you here?"

Walter was an intimidating presence. He dwarfed Rebecca, his head grazing the top of the doorway. He wasn't a particularly unattractive man on first glance, except for the tattoo of an eagle's wings enveloping his neck like a stranglehold. Rebecca's co-workers would have understood what she saw in him. Only those who really got to know Walter could have recognized how his unappealing personality distorted his physical features. Rebecca was still repulsed, three years later.

"Still go for the older men I see," Walter remarked, noticing Atom in the car.

"I know me being here is a little random, but I need your help. Can I switch cars with you for the weekend?"

Walter grinned devilishly. "You meanin' to trade your hunk a junk for the beauty I got in the garage here? What's in it for me?"

"I'm in a lot of trouble. I need to disappear for a little while, but I can't do that in my car."

"Your boyfriend can't help you none?" Walter said, referencing Atom.

"He's not my boyfriend." Rebecca sounded desperate and scared. Her plea for help was genuine.

"What kind a trouble did you get your pretty little self into?" Walter was playing games. He did not take Rebecca seriously. Never did.

"I don't have time to explain. You won't understand."

"Ways I see it, I don't have to give you nothin'."

Walter collected an impressive wad of phlegm in his throat and spit it out onto the adjacent rosebush.

"I forgot how disgusting you are," Rebecca said.

There were many things about Walter she did not remember until she journeyed back to the scenes of the crime. She fell into the trap of remembering Walter by the disingenuous stories of him she would tell others, like the other nurses, so she didn't appear to be the lonesome desperate loser she knew she was. The concocted memories were much more tolerable and were the perfect remedy of the past.

Rebecca made a huge mistake. If only Atom was healthy enough to talk some sense into her. Instead, she further complicated the situation by involving her perverted ex. As she held onto the railing for balance in the shadow of Walter's stature, Rebecca wondered how she could have ever been attracted to him.

Youth and vulnerability would be appropriate excuses for her poor judgment. She embodied both of those traits when they met at the Crow's Nest. Despite his uneducated drawl, Walter possessed one appealing characteristic that Atom could never match. He was competitive at the Guess Who board game.

They shared memories over drinks, Rebecca happy to finally have somebody she could confide in. Walter's charm lasted as long as Atom's crooked span of attention. He was no confidant. Atom was a much better listener with twice the brains.

None of that mattered as Rebecca tried to escape from Walter a second time.

"I made a big mistake coming here," she confessed, slowly backing away from Walter's reach. "I'm sorry for taking up your time."

"Now hold it a sec here," Walter barked, freezing Rebecca in her tracks. "You laid a deal out on the table. I don't remember you taking back no deal."

Rebecca sensed trouble brewing. Walter only helped others if it benefited his own cause. She nervously waited for the verdict.

"Don't it seem a little one-sided in your favor?" Walter continued. "I'm gonna need something extra for me to accept your offer. Something *special.*"

Walter smiled and licked his lips.

Rebecca's heart lost all hope in humanity. It was trying to suffocate itself in her throat to leave behind a world of hatred and despair. Rebecca should have expected such a proposition from Walter. How desperate was she? Could she take her chances with Atom in her car or was she powerless to Walter's demands?

Rebecca turned and saw Atom sitting in her car, reciting Humphrey Bogart's lines like a caged parrot trained in imitation. She broke down in tears.

How did she not learn from her past?

"You are a mind numbing, crippling disease," Rebecca said. "I want to forget the moment I saw you. I'm leaving."

"You know you ain't goin' nowhere," Walter expressed. "You don't need me tellin' people where you been in your car. Come on upstairs and we can discuss a little more about that deal of yours you proposed. Maybe we can come to an agreement."

Rebecca had no options. If she did, she would have never come. She needed his car more than she needed her pride. There was nobody else she could turn to.

I'm doing this for Atom, Rebecca tried to convince herself.

"You'll love driving my baby," Walter said, as he waved Rebecca into his house. "It's got so many amenities. But I'm gonna need to test drive your goods first."

Rebecca reluctantly stepped inside and followed him upstairs, wishing the rusted railing wasn't so damn supportive. Another memorable moment for the lonely nurse. Another unsigned permission slip for a trip into the wilderness without anybody's consent. This time, it wasn't a family vacation.

Her plan wasn't going as planned.

"It's not safe, coat hangers and rags. Life is sacred. We can make it together," Atom continued from the car with his self-treatment to Alzheimer's.

CHAPTER SIX

Jason did not know how to dance. On a sliding scale, he would rate himself a three out of 10 with 10 being his grandmother blindfolded on stilts. To be fair, Jason's grandmother was better known for her best-selling line of Dutch oven cookbooks, another reason why Jason had no business outliving his name.

Preserving the influential Strykowski cooking reputation far outweighed killing off the clumsy Strykowski dancing gene. However, the online questionnaire didn't ask any culinary skills. Jason compensated by selecting *above average,* hoping that he wouldn't have to provide visual evidence at the next local square dancing event.

If I could dance, I wouldn't be filling this out, Jason mused.

Speed dating was a bust. Jason thought the next

logical step in finding a loveless relationship was via online dating. It was the perfect platform for the impersonal and the passive. Jason fell into both categories. Users wouldn't even have to meet their computer-generated matches. A 30 day free trial, a cute username, an inaccurate profile picture, and a deceitful questionnaire was the closest he'd be required to get to his compatibility results. If only making a baby was that easy.

Jason proceeded to the next page of questions.

I am a dreamer - Yes   No   Sometimes

He didn't understand the question. The previous night he dreamed he was wearing one of those pet collars that funnel up over the head. People kept calling his name, but he couldn't turn to see whom they were. Jason wasn't sure if that qualified for answering the vague dream question in the affirmative. He selected the *sometimes* option. A safe decision, so he couldn't be held accountable.

The multiple-choice section of the test was over. Jason was relieved. The more interesting short-answer portion followed. This was where he hoped to stand out; however, the first question had him stumped.

Describe yourself in 250 words or less.

This was harder than passing the Bar exam. Jason already completed the difficult task of reducing his existence into 25 multiple-choice answers, which would have been easier if there were a few *all of the above* options. Now he was asked to expound his 45 years into five short essays totaling less than 1,250 words. He was a more complex subject than he initially gave himself credit for. If this were a test, Jason might be failing. He already got the dancing question wrong and the one about being a dreamer was a complete guess. He needed to do some last minute studying to salvage his grade.

Jason opened up a new window on his computer and went to Google. It took the search engine fifteen-tenths of a second to unearth 157,000 results for a search of his last name. Google thought the Strykowski's were popular. Not quite on the same cyber plane as Lincoln, but popular nonetheless. Jason perused the search results of his family. His uncle, P.J. Strykowski, dominated the first page with links to his widely accepted publications on mechanical engineering. His cousin, Nicole Strykowski, also made front-page Google news with her award-winning performance as Keely in *Keely and Du.* Over a half dozen links focused on the accomplishments of his aunt as the first female president of the Danish National Space Center in the department of Geodynamics.

The press for his family went on and on, not to mention the rich Strykowski history. How was Jason to compress the information in less than 250 words? If he copy and pasted info about himself from the websites, would that be considered plagiarism? Jason concluded that he was probably failing the test anyway.

Buried 15 colored O's deep, Jason found a few of the criminal cases that he tried. It saddened him to realize that he wasn't able to contribute more to the family tradition other than the few undeserving people he helped put behind bars. There was a small Associated Press article recognizing the incestuous pedophile he was currently defending, but Jason's name was misspelled and it didn't paint him in a favorable light for having such a twisted client. He wasn't a war hero like his grandfather or an actor like his cousin. He couldn't cook like his grandmother or live up to the moral standard of his father. The Strykowski's were a musically inclined family for at least seven generations, Jason's great-great grandfather reaching the pinnacle of the profession by playing with the New York Philharmonic for three years as a cellist. Jason had no musical abilities.

Maybe I'm adopted, Jason joked. *Wouldn't that be ironic?*

One hundred and fifty-seven thousand web pages. There was no way Jason could sift through his entire family history in one sitting. Would the last event that Google ever recognizes about the Strykowski's be Jason's obituary?

The more research Jason conducted, the more he accepted his assignment. He had to make a sacrifice for the greater good. He still didn't want to have to stoop to the mushy sentiments that normally establish a relationship to complete his goal. It wasn't in his character and he hated being phony. Besides, a heart wasn't meant to be broken more than once. Jason wouldn't be able to survive another attack, or so he convinced himself for more than 20 years.

Describe yourself in 250 words or less.

After the Google probing, Jason only needed one word to answer the question. The web pages he was looking for about himself had not yet been established.

Unfinished. That was the adjective he best felt described himself.

Summing up his story as if it were a movie log line was a challenge he now welcomed. Jason's online dating profile was turning into a force to be reckoned with, even if it was a little disingenuous. His profile picture was 20 years old and 15 pounds ago. In the general information section, he spotted himself five extra inches and 10 percent more hair. These white lies were designed to generate more hits for his profile. If Jason's online dating game ever made it to the physical realm, he would have a lot of explaining to do. It would probably be easier for him to wear a rug on his head and stilts on his feet to match the personal information he submitted. He could then go stilt dancing with his grandmother. If all else failed, he'd have all 157,000 Google results printed out to bring with him on his date to seal the deal. If she were going to bear the next Strykowski child, Jason would have to win her over with his impressive bloodline.

You would be the mother of a very impressive son, he imagined pitching.

That was the plan all along.

The exam was over. He completed the remaining short answers as if he were filling out Mad Libs, delivering inventive adjectives to describe the story of his life. After clicking save, a pop-up screen infested the computer monitor.

CONGRATULATIONS!
You've just won a GPS for your travels! Click HERE to retrieve your prize.

Jason assumed the pop-up was an advertisement. He came across similar windows in the past and never once pursued the bait. *CONGRATULATIONS* continuously flashed red, enticing an otherwise uninterested consumer.

Being a lawyer, Jason looked for the fine print; something to tell him that his winnings were only valid in North Dakota on the autumnal equinox. With a magnifying glance, he could not find any small print. Odds were likely that if he followed the link to receive his free GPS, he'd either be redirected to another advertisement or inadvertently download a computer virus. Jason's inquisitiveness cheered him on to take the chance. The retail price of the GPS pictured was at least $400. If he did in fact win one for filling out an online personal survey, he wouldn't let the opportunity to save go to waste. He had little use for a GPS. Rarely did he travel farther than his own town, but anything free was worth the price.

The mouse hovered over the link. Jason contemplated his curiosity one last time before clicking his way to a complimentary technological wonder. A sub page opened asking for Jason's shipping information.

Did it work? Jason hoped. He was still waiting for the catch. There was always a catch, like having to purchase anything over $1,500 for the free GPS. It wasn't asking for any billing information though. There was no space to enter a credit card number or a PayPal account.

Jason entered in his personal information, this time without stretching the truth. He had no one to impress.

"What's the worst that can happen?" Jason asked himself. It didn't occur to him that he might be giving away his home address to a gang of high-tech thieves. He submitted the info and didn't spontaneously combust. He survived.

Jason just won himself a $400 GPS for his car.

I'll use it when I go on my dates, Jason planned.

When he was finished exploiting himself in cyberspace, Jason closed all the windows to Internet

Explorer, revealing his desktop picture, which displayed a plain faced teenage beauty with her head resting on a younger Jason's right shoulder. Jason stared longingly through the photo for a brief time. It was his reminder of a broken heart. She was Jason's excuse for his endangered existence. He touched the screen affectionately, but the resulting sparks were only from the static charge.

A beat later, Jason turned the power off and watched the desktop picture disappear. The screen went black.

Jason was alone. What else was new?

CHAPTER SEVEN

Norman felt uninspired by his territory. He was always assigned to the affluent neighborhoods, harboring houses that already had maid service or vacuums capable of picking up million dollar baby droppings and $300 red wine stains. Norman was competent at guessing the houses boasting hardwood floors that were only in the market for a mop and a bucket of water. He didn't waste his time on those houses. Norman was selective in his approach; the sales experts would have opined he was too selective, reciting the motto *a sale waits in every corner.* However, as long as he sold one vacuum a day, he could pay for gas and another night at a hotel with complimentary breakfast in the morning. That was his modus operandi for several years, and he was good at it, too. He had to be. His personality interfered with his ability to sell multiple units at one time, but Norman didn't care.

It wasn't always vacuum cleaners. There was a five-year span when he sold multi-colored splashguards for urinals. They say you are what you sell. Norman was a target for being pissed on regularly. He toured restaurants and bars all across the country. Nobody took him or his product seriously.

"I guess you like to have piss stains on your pants when you leave the bathroom," he'd say to any disinterested customer.

At a hole in the wall outside of Indianapolis, Norman snapped. After hearing a bar full of drunks call him a piss catcher and spit beer on his shoes, he decided it was time to show these crapulent assholes how his product worked. Free of charge. He located the most vocal buffoon and greeted him with a right hook to the jaw. The bar rat staggered back before crashing to the floor. He was knocked out cold.

The bar was quiet. Norman had their attention.

He turned the unconscious man over on his back with his beer soaked shoe and tossed a bright pink splashguard onto his emotionless face.

"Now, gentlemen, notice how I can cut down on what I like to call urinary scatter," Norman said, as he unzipped his fly.

The crowd was stunned as they watched Norman urinate all over the defenseless guy's face right in front of the bar by the restaurant entrance. Any passersby window-shopping would catch an unexpected surprise. When Norman finished, he zipped up and faced the stunned onlookers.

"My pants are completely dry," Norman said.

Mr. Dry Pants left without saying another word.

A year later, to the day, in a coincident bar in another unfamiliar town, Norman was forced to make another public display to prove his sales pitch worthy. But this time, with his pants around his ankles and a bar full of drunks providing their undivided attention, waiting for the opportunity to pounce the arrogant salesman, Norman's pecker decided to go on strike. No relief. No discharge. The plan backfired, and for the first time, the man in the room with his pants pulled down fulfilled the proper role of being the brunt of the joke, the tragic actor in the scene. Norman was humiliated. Vulnerable. The bar rat on the floor wearing the splashguard like a gasmask pulled out a knife and sprung up on Norman. He would never have a comfortable piss again, and little use for his product. However, that would be the least of his problems.

That was the last time he attempted to sell multi-colored splashguards. He was tired of being pissed on.

He felt more comfortable being pissed off. He wore that mask permanently.

I gotta get out of this neighborhood, Norman thought. He wasn't going to sell any vacuums driving up and down the privileged cul-de-sacs where every house was Art Deco with marble driveways and three swimming pools. These suburban aristocrats probably had a vacuum in every walk-in closet. The target markets for the Power Hum Vac 3500X lived on the outskirts of this high-class community, where carpet friendly country-folk escaped from the north and pigpen metropolitans threatened from the south.

Norman pulled over to the side of the road and

reached into the backseat for his road atlas. He pushed aside his suitcase and vacuum like a true friend. As he blindly groped for the map among everything else littering his backseat, including outdated newspapers and three-week-old fast food doggy bags, he remembered Gloria's bestowment. It sat on the passenger's seat still enclosed in its packaging.

Out of spite, Norman did not want to use it. Gloria would win if he did. Her gift was a most selfish act of charity. Operating it would mean he would accept her therapy.

Nobody gets me, Norman professed. Just like Annabelle Lwin at a candy store, he could not resist the temptation. Without further self-prodding, he decided to assemble the GPS to prove that it would not have any changing effect on him. He would remain the miserable piss catcher he always was.

Norman stared down at the GPS box, rereading the tag line: *The perfect companion for when you don't know where you're going!* The slogan made him chuckle.

"All right, I'll follow you."

He tore apart the box and unveiled the GPS. The color monitor was no bigger than the size of his palm. Norman was disappointed, expecting a larger screen, perhaps a 35-inch plasma. It was in his nature to anticipate the impossible. It was the only way to feed his disappointment. He plugged the power adapter into the cigarette lighter and attached the GPS to the opposite end of the cord.

The screen came to life.

Technology did not agree with Norman. He never could figure out how to unlock the adult content channels on the television sets in his hotel rooms and he constantly had to make the awkward phone call to the front desk for help. It was a wonder he could turn on his vacuum cleaner. The appliance never returned the favor.

As the main menu loaded on Norman's new toy, he flipped through the directions hastily to learn the settings.

"To plan your first route, follow the steps below," Norman recited from the quick start guide. "Tap the screen to bring up the main menu and then tap on the *Navigate To* icon to begin entering an address."

Norman tried tapping the screen. Nothing happened. He pressed a little harder. Still no response. The GPS displayed the time and date by the left corner of the screen. A compass was situated to the bottom left. The signal strength and battery power flashed across the top of the screen above a dormant computerized map of Norman's current location, his car represented by a small triangular icon. No matter where on the screen Norman tapped, he could not awaken a menu.

Below the first step in the quick start guide was a self-proclaimed important notice to the user: *You should always plan your trip before you start driving. It is dangerous to plan a route while driving.*

Norman was already confused. How special was this GPS if it had him lost while reading the directions? It wasn't living up to the tag line on the box. Giving up, Norman tossed the directions aside and shifted his car out of park.

"I have no time for this."

His 15-year-old book of U.S. maps didn't need to be programmed or plugged in. Just flip to the desired state or city and plan out a route the old-fashioned way. It didn't contain the latest maps, but it never steered Norman in the wrong direction. Maybe that was his problem. There was only one catch though.

What state am I in again?

He couldn't remember; a momentary brain fart to loosen a little of his constipated mental state. Norman had been on the road with no destination most of his life, rarely paying attention to the borders he crossed. The license plates on the cars passing by were a reminder of his present coordinates.

Driving with one hand on the wheel and one eye on the road, Norman tried to find the most direct route out of the nauseating upper class community on page 38 of his road atlas and into the more economically tolerant city on page 39 and 40. What a difference one page makes.

Norman looked for a sign. Any sign.

"After one-quarter mile, turn left," a female voice with a British accent interrupted.

"Excuse me?"

Taken by surprise, he didn't know what else to say. "I'm hearing voices," he continued, re-evaluating his sanity like a quarterback on the line weary of the defense's formation. He drove past an industrial complex on his left and a community swimming pool on his right. Both were insignificant landmarks for the road atlas to have documented. Norman was lost physically and mentally.

"Turn left now," the female voice prompted.

She was coming from Gloria's GPS. The screen came to life with mesmerizing colors and was tracking Norman's travels on an interactive map that was so accurate, it even displayed the passing industrial complex and community swimming pool. The road atlas felt so inadequate that it fell to the floor and considered the future of print. A bright red left turn arrow blinked on the screen as it showed Norman the approaching intersection. Confusion gave way to panic as he reached the pivotal crossroad. Norman had to make a decision. Quick. A yellow or red light did not provide Norman with the opportunity to deliberate the GPS's unsought command. Without giving himself a chance to weigh his options, Norman felt pressured to comply with the strange request for no better reason than it being the only advice he had. Instead of continuing straight, he made a left onto a residential road, just like the GPS said.

Norman tried to make sense of the situation as he drove down the new street, his GPS mimicking his every move. He wasn't savvy with electronics, but he knew that a GPS had to be programmed for it to be able to provide any directions. Unlike Gloria, it was no mind reader.

"Defective piece of shit," Norman barked. He was angrier with himself for momentarily giving Gloria the benefit of the doubt than at the malfunctioning device.

"After one-quarter mile, turn right," the GPS directed.

Tapping on the screen did nothing to override the unwanted assistance. Even if he knew how, Norman didn't have a destination to provide the machine.

Less than 500 feet in front of him was the entrance onto the turnpike. He would have to make the GPS' requested right turn in order to take it going east.

Where is it taking me?

The turnpike stretched across three states. If he followed the GPS' directions, he could be traveling to any number of destinations.

"Turn right now," it reminded him, as he approached the stop sign.

He could have easily made another left and headed west. A second option was to stay local by continuing with the road he was currently on. He could have also unplugged the presumptuous GPS and paved his own path. He didn't know where to go. At least the GPS seemed to be confident. It didn't hurt that the voice instructing him was female. It made him feel desired. No longer alone. For once in his life, Norman was more comfortable following directions with no destination, rather than having the destination without direction.

A red right turn arrow blinked on the screen, waiting for Norman's decision.

"Fuck it," he said. Norman turned right.

The GPS recalculated and remained quiet as Norman merged. Norman wondered when he was going to make his next turn. He passed a sign for a rest stop as he increased his speed to respectable highway travel. The next sign read *Next Exit - 30 miles*, which made him a bit unsure of his decision to pursue the unknown.

There goes lunch, Norman grumbled. There were probably some three-week-old leftovers in the backseat to hold him over.

The small triangle impersonating Norman's car continued to glide along a satellite rendering of the turnpike. The GPS was silent and wouldn't have anything to say for at least 30 miles. Norman missed her voice already.

To speed up the process, Norman nudged on the accelerator.

Norman didn't realize, but he and the Power Hum Vac 3500X were being abducted, and Norman was the pilot.

CHAPTER EIGHT

Sickness will surely take the mind where minds won't usually go.

Rebecca needed to work on her transitions. She went from being at the nursing home with a concrete plan, to screwing her ex-boyfriend in exchange for his car.

At the top of a Ferris wheel with her forgetful sidekick, a dying man 30 years her senior, no longer with a plan, Rebecca was unraveling as slowly as the rotating ride she couldn't escape from.

She tried to understand how she arrived at the amusement park. The only explanation she could reach was that Walter's car had a mind of its own. Walter was right. His Audi came equipped with several amenities, one of them being a built-in GPS that was as misguided as Atom's memories. Rebecca thought she plugged in the address for MIT to reintroduce Atom to his past, which she followed turn for turn; however, the car brought her to a much different destination. If Rebecca had not just been violated, she may have realized that the directions were suspect halfway into her trip. She wasn't concentrating. The carnival tents and the cotton candy stands were her only indication during her two-hour drive that she did not reach the University. Walter's car seemed to suffer from the same affliction as Atom. Rebecca blamed herself for trusting anything that Walter owned.

Atom appeared comfortable and at home as they pulled into the parking lot, as if this was right where he wanted to be. If Atom didn't have Alzheimer's, he may have remembered MIT as a three-ring circus. From what Rebecca deducted from Atom's murky past, Atom and his scientific findings were not taken very seriously. He was treated like a clown.

Maybe this is where we're supposed to be, Rebecca wondered.

It took Rebecca the entire two-hour drive to temporarily expunge the memory from her eyes of the 15 minutes she spent in Walter's bedroom. She was all out of emotion by the time the GPS incorrectly told her that she reached her destination. Hunger was her only prevailing feeling. The only thing she had all day was half a cup of tea. There must have been something to suppress her appetite in the park while she attempted to regain her bearings.

The GPS only provided her with the choice of exploration, so she left the car to explore the unexpected carnival destination.

"Does this place look familiar to you?" She wondered if she took Atom to a landmark in his past.

He did not respond, not even as Humphrey Bogart.

"Can you remember? Please tell me that you remember."

They passed all types of rides and games, lights and buzzers. Atom was mesmerized by the scene, much like the children waiting in line to board the bumper cars and the roller coaster. He was soaking it all in, but like an abused and overused sponge, Atom couldn't hold his water. Rebecca would not be distracted from fulfilling her appetite. As they passed the house of mirrors and the difficult ring tossing game, Rebecca noticed a police officer approaching.

Could he be looking for me? Rebecca wondered. She knew it was impossible. Her car was hibernating safely in Walter's garage. Only the GPS knew where she was. Not even Atom could divulge Rebecca's whereabouts, and he was right there with her. Still, the sight of the authority figure made her panic. She grabbed Atom and cut back down the alley toward the Ferris wheel. She turned back and in some way was relieved to see the officer randomly looking around through his thick black glasses as if he were a lost, abandoned child. Rebecca tried to convince herself that he had nothing to do with her. She couldn't take the chance. She pulled Atom in line for the Ferris wheel just as they were loading it for the next ride. They waited impatiently, with Rebecca's one eye glued to the cop.

Rebecca nudged the family in front of them to move faster down the line. The spots on the wheel were filling up quickly. According to her unofficial calculations, they were right on the cusp of either making it on or having to wait in line for another turn. She couldn't afford to stay on the ground. Just the sight of the uniformed man in blue made the repercussions of being caught that much more realistic and frightening.

The police officer wasn't leaving and anyone guilty of anything would have been suspicious of his presence. Rebecca was paranoid. The Ferris wheel operator had the loading process stalled as he measured a little girl's height up against a cardboard cutout of a smiling clown, her brother tormenting her to tears.

A familiar scene.

Rebecca lost any patience she had in the reserve.

"Excuse me, we need to get on," Rebecca said while squeezing past the family in front of her waiting for the little girl to pass the height test.

"You can wait your turn," the little girl's mother replied with an attitude.

Rebecca introduced Atom to the snotty mother trying to smuggle her underage daughter onto the ride. "I've got a handicapped Vet here," she said, using Atom as her ticket away from the cop and to the front of the line where a bitter old man with one arm operating the mechanical wheel from an outdoor glass cubicle collected money from the people waiting to ride.

"Two tickets, please."

Rebecca handed the one-armed man exact change, wishing she reserved her comment about Atom being handicapped in front of him. For some strange reason, she felt sad for the carnie missing one appendage, but she did not have time to offer him a hand.

"Don't trust a man with one hand!" Atom shouted.

"What did you say?" Rebecca responded, hope gleaming from her tone, assured there was a dose of judgment in Atom's statement.

"How can you study the guidelines of the future without first descending down the tracks of the past?" Atom continued. "Where is the other hand? How can we judge?"

"What are you trying to tell me?"

"Excuse me, we're all waiting," the mother in line behind Atom and Rebecca grunted. Her children were growing restless, brother and sister climbing on top of one another, the cardboard clown supervising the monkey business.

Rebecca and Atom were pushed passed the one-armed carnie, the weight of the mother and law forcing them forward toward the wheel like two blind mice in need of some brainless exercise.

Six dollars later, they were sitting on the bottom capsule of the Ferris wheel waiting for the one-armed man to commence liftoff.

"What did you say before?" Rebecca asked. "Can you say it again?"

"Jackknives and army ants play situational comedies after a night of rewriting the rule book," Atom noted, accompanied by his usual smile. "Polyester personalities critique their kin."

The Alzheimer's was talking again. Rebecca was exhausted. The Alzheimer's never ceased talking. She should have known better than to get her hopes up. She should have still been preoccupied with the circus cop's predatory presence.

If the flatfoot were really there for Rebecca, he would have apprehended her already, unless he was really as lost as he appeared. Rebecca, in her haste, sought refuse on the wheel, a poor choice, if another escape was required.

She felt guilty for having to involve Atom. He didn't seem to mind though. They sat across from one another in a small booth, their thoughts miles apart.

Suddenly, the Ferris wheel jockeyed out of park and spun them upward.

Rebecca faced opposite the rotation of the wheel, just as she preferred, to help guide her thoughts in a comfortable direction away from all other influences forging forward. She was taken back to the first time she and her brother ever visited a theme park. They were no older than 9 or 10 years old, before such establishments practiced height discrimination for entry onto the rides. She remembered winning a stuffed giraffe and glow-in-the-dark sunglasses for being the best at handling a water pistol while staring down the open mouth of her red-nosed enemy jester.

As Rebecca recollected, she smiled. Her memory of that day was too vivid not to share it with Atom, who, according to Rebecca's professional nursing opinion, was desperately searching for a memory of his own to get lost in. He never heard this particular story about her past before. Rebecca didn't need to take it out of her cerebral storage facility to grapple with until she found herself atop a Ferris wheel hiding out from the authority below.

"Dad told us to wait in this really long line while he went for… um, food," Rebecca narrated for Atom, who was blind to the flashback playing in Rebecca's private theater. "They said they'd be right back. I held my brother's hand and we waited, the line growing longer behind us without it compensating for its unsuspected growth spurt at the stagnant front. We didn't move from our original position for 20 minutes. The people in line in front of us were getting impatient."

Back in reality, Atom's universe, Rebecca and Atom's cell reached the top of the ride, completing one-half revolution around the circumference of the wheel. Rebecca did not push pause on the remote controlling her memory to enjoy the descending aerial view. She continued to look back.

"We didn't know where the line snaked. It was too long, we were too short, and it wrapped around several different tents and kiosks, all factors working together to prevent us from seeing the front everybody wanted to approach. Twenty minutes pass and the line starts moving. We didn't know what to do. Our parents told us to stay put, but the people behind my brother and me kept telling us to move up."

Rebecca momentarily suspended her storytelling as they reached the bottom of the Ferris wheel so she could concentrate on the faces in the crowd. One full revolution complete. She could no longer locate the policeman. She felt both relieved and unsettled at the same time as they were vaulted upward for a second go-around on the repetitive ride. Like her story to Atom, they were going nowhere.

"We finally make it to the beginning of the line. Halfway across the carnival from where our parents told us to stay and suddenly..."

The Ferris wheel stopped moving, jolting Rebecca out of her comfortable past. Their world swung gently with the breeze at the pinnacle of the wheel's height. Atom and Rebecca were stuck 200 feet above the ground.

"We seem to be having some technical difficulties," a voice ripped through a megaphone to reach those suspended above. "Everybody stay calm and we will have you down in no time."

Can this day get any worse? Rebecca wondered.

The world looked so small atop her perch. The carnival-goers infested the ground like mice and she was the lone hawk patrolling the skies for her prey. She had her talons out for the cop. He was gone.

Other riders were beginning to get restless. Rebecca was no exception. She couldn't enjoy being in the moment, but Atom was on top of the world. He smiled at the setting sun and relaxed into a comfortable gaze. Unlike Rebecca and the sun, he was in no hurry to descend.

"Soggy Cocoa Puffs walk the fields of grain," Atom said softly.

What a sad, sick man, Rebecca thought. She had a few tears left in the reserve to produce for Atom's wellbeing. She cried for two. He smiled for none. They shared the same moment differently.

"I'm going to help you. I promise."

Fifteen minutes passed without a resolution to the technical difficulties. Rebecca located Walter's car in the carnival parking lot, the most unlikely of vehicles impelling her into the future for Atom's past. The navigation system that was responsible for trapping her on top of the Ferris wheel must have been laughing away at Rebecca's unfortunate situation. She needed to escape. Again.

She thought about starting her story over to Atom from the beginning, but she knew it didn't matter. She had to finish the story for her own sake. As the world around her remained stagnant, she continued where she left off.

"So, my brother and I make it to the front of the line and suddenly..."

CHAPTER NINE

Jason Strykowski's day took an unexpected left turn. Literally. He was driving down I-35, doing 75 in the right lane, when his prize-winning navigation system told him to take the rapidly approaching exit to his left without prior warning. The address on his mystery date's online profile said she lived in Briarcliff, but the city name on the exit sign advertised Worton Heights, which to Jason's understanding, was five miles west of Briarcliff. Relying on the wonders of technology over that of human reason, Jason thought it would be best to follow the GPS' instructions.

With no more than 500 yards to the exit ramp, Jason had to cross two lanes while avoiding the deadly four-wheeled obstacles moving in and out of his way in order to comply with the GPS' hasty request. He sped up to cut in front of a garbage truck in the middle lane.

"Take the exit left now."

A blue Camry in the left lane driving at a comparable speed had Jason boxed out of shifting over. The man behind the wheel was oblivious to Jason's left turn signal. Their vehicles were perfectly parallel to each other as they raced down I-35.

"This fucking guy," Jason remarked, as he honked the horn to get his attention. According to the GPS, he had exactly 250 yards before the exit. He didn't have anymore time to waste, especially at his current speed. Slowing down and pulling behind the inattentive car in the left lane was not an option because the garbage truck was riding his ass, probably because Jason cut him off. The yellow sign on the grille of the garbage truck, which read, DANGER - Large Load, appeared much bigger than it actually was through the rearview mirror. He had to risk speeding up and overshooting the exit in order to take the left lane.

How much faster could he go? He was already well into the eighties according to the speedometer, and he didn't know if his 10-year old Subaru could handle anymore excitement.

"In one hundred yards, take the exit left," the GPS reminded casually.

The nose of Jason's Subaru inched ahead of its drag racing opponent as it shook itself to 90 miles per hour. He was still unsure whether he had enough room to cut in front. Either the other driver was consciously preventing Jason from making his move or he was oblivious to the world around him and was determined to stay his course.

The two drivers were afforded a momentary glimpse

at one another as their machines rocketed them forward at the same speed. Jason saw himself. Not really. The man piloting the Camry was much older and sported a long, gray beard, but the man hogging the left lane echoed the physical characteristics of Jason's mental state. There was an immediate connection, as if their two cars were meant to remain parallel forever. In that moment, neither driver was lost, but something urged them apart, and Jason, as well as his reflection in the other car, was under its spell.

"Take the exit right now."

If Jason was to make his move, he had to act fast. A safer option would have been to turn around at the next exit, but he did not know how many miles that would be. Without any time to make further rationalization, he swerved into the left lane, taking a chance on his life. If he didn't have the other car's attention before, he certainly had it now. The blue Camry let out a loud, sustained honk as its brakes locked and screeched. Barely avoiding Jason and the tailgating garbage truck, the blue Camry righted itself and continued on its voyage. By the time order was restored to the highway, Jason had already taken both the left lane and the adjoining exit, all in one maneuver. He must have given the blue Camry a big scare. He was pretty shaken up himself, sweat dripping from his brow and moistening his palms.

"At the end of the road, turn right," the GPS said in its most assuaging voice, as if it wasn't flustered or impressed with the near death experience it created.

"You're trying to kill me."

Jason complied with the navigator's latest direction at a much safer speed. This time, he was given ample time to prepare for the right turn off the exit ramp.

Jason drove through a nice neighborhood, affluence on prominent display. He passed various antique storefronts and fancy outdoor restaurants while creeping down Worton Heights' cobblestone main street. It was a quaint town, a perfect Sunday afternoon getaway. Couples were enjoying each other's company over lunch and window-shopping down the sidewalks, a cynical sight for Jason indeed.

"After twenty yards, you have reached your destination."

HugsNKisses35 did not live 20 yards away. That was his date's online profile name. Jason's new GPS let him down, and almost killed him in the process.

"No wonder you were free."

Jason passed a bookstore on his right and the Worton Heights Library on his left. He laughed at the poor location of the bookstore. An establishment offered the same product for free right across the street.

"You have reached your destination."

Jason slowed to a stop at the intersection of Main and Prince Street. He didn't need to reference the address flashing on the navigator to figure out where it wanted him to be, which wasn't his date's studio apartment in Briarcliff. Not yet at least.

Jason's impromptu destination was Delia's Flower Boutique.

"Is this a sick joke? What, did my mother program this GPS?"

In spite of his mother's recommendation, he didn't understand the attraction of handing someone a bouquet of dying foliage. To him, flowers were weeds. How did something that animals piss on become an object of love?

That four-letter word. Jason may have thought picking flowers to be a nonsensical ritual, but the real reason why he feared presenting his date with flowers was to avoid having to be mixed up in the aforementioned four-letter word. He didn't want to give his date any false signals. Love was a fatal disease, easily contagious that could be spread with something as simple as a rose or a tulip.

Jason had already been infected.

This was just a business trip, and all that he needed was his research and the cold, hard facts. His bouquet was a stapled packet of the top 10 Strykowski Google results.

"You have reached your destination," the GPS reminded, as if coercing Jason to check out the special sales inside Delia's Flower Boutique. The sign above the door was written with flowers to drive home the theme within.

I can't believe she stooped this low, Jason thought, accusing his mother of reprogramming his GPS to the flower shop. It was a much more concrete theory than blaming the navigation system for being defective. Again, Jason was taking the side of technology over humanity. It was also possible that the online dating service he won the navigation system from partnered with many flower shops, candy stores, and greeting card outlets around the country and preprogrammed their information into their free GPS product for a flat advertising fee. It would be an ingenious association. The retailers would be guaranteeing themselves a high conversion rate of potential customers to actual customers. They'd be directed right to their doorstep.

Jason didn't give the corporate world that much credit to accept the last theory as a possibility. He would much rather blame his mother.

Jason contemplated driving away from Delia's shop, standing up his blind date, and forfeiting the mission to find the incubator who would salvage the Strykowski name. He'd do it out of spite to get back at his mother for pulling such a juvenile act. However, he remembered his father's dying wishes, the purity in his sickly voice when he used up his final moments to explain the importance of Jason's choices for the future.

"Come here my boy," Mr. Strykowski said to his only son while laying on a hospital bed preparing to escape a lifetime of pain...for good.

Jason stood by the door not sure how he should react in front of his dying father. Should he recognize the gravity of the situation and acknowledge death as the three-ton elephant in the room? Or should he act as if everything was perfectly normal so that he didn't create unnecessary doubts about the inevitable? He chose the latter to deflect the sobriety of the situation by convincing himself that this would not be their final encounter. Their final conversation. Jason approached cautiously, expecting to get the predictable lecture on his purpose in life and how it would be selfish of him not to pursue what was best for the family. He already made the decision not to marry and refused to believe that his last one-on-one with his father would be another marketing ploy to sell the importance of preserving the great Strykowski name.

"The past is the past. We all make mistakes. We both made mistakes. We both forgot what was best for the family. I am so proud of you and whatever you decide your life to be is what is meant to be."

Although what the dying man said wasn't true, it meant a great deal to Jason, who had to put up with everybody telling him how to live his life, including his father. They were so relentless. The life they painted for him became so unappealing for no specific reason other than it was what all of his critics selfishly rooted to see fulfilled. But the night of his father's passing, Jason had control of his fate for the first time. And for the first time, the prospect of becoming a father was no longer out of the question. It just needed to be his decision, and only his decision.

"...and I am so proud to be your father."

Jason held onto his hand and cried. He wondered if he would ever get to say those same words. On a day when he was supposed to be making his sick father more comfortable, Jason was the one being soothed.

His mother was right after all, or so Jason thought. He feared he might have indirectly killed his father, encouraged his disease, because of his selfish behavior.

"You have reached your destination," the GPS interrupted.

"Stupid piece of junk!" Jason yelled, turning the navigator off. He couldn't understand why it would keep reiterating his destination. How did it know he was still in the car? Does a GPS left alone in the car make a noise?

Jason was no longer sure if his memory of his dying father was completely accurate anymore. It didn't matter. He liked the distorted version better. It paved a clearer path into the future.

Jason's newest disruption came in the form of a knock on his driver's side window. Morphing with the faint reflection of his own countenance was an old man's wrinkled face staring back at him from the other side of the window. He was holding a fresh bouquet of bright yellow flowers, Delia's latest sale. The brightness they evoked made up for his slowly losing grip on a smile.

"Stop following me," the strange man behind the window said. "The flowers are for Mommy."

Jason was taken aback and looked to his GPS for direction.

"Sorry about this," the caretaker to the old man said, as she approached Jason's car for an informal introduction to the predestined encounter. "He has Alzheimer's."

She ushered him away along with his flowers and his sorry excuse for a smile.

"Leave me alone to trade Q-tips for plungers, so I can scratch and scrape at the fox's hound."

Jason didn't know what to make of the confrontation. He changed his mind back to the task at hand.

"You have reached your destination," the GPS reminded.

The transplanted pots of snapdragons and white carnations by the fence cried out for sympathy. The blue delphiniums guarding the doorway aspired to welcome new life into the world. The lilies and daisy poms beyond Delia's storefront window said, "Get well," to the inflicted and, "Stay well," to the healthy.

Jason sat in his car weighing his options. He decided to enter the flower shop. He would ask if they could recommend a flower that would communicate, "I want to be the father of your son."

CHAPTER TEN

The circus was in their rearview mirror. Rebecca drove in silence; thoughts of Atom's condition occupying her mind's time.

She knew how it worked scientifically. Memories are enhanced patterns of neuronal interconnections. Every bit of data filtered through our senses are encoded, stored, and then retrieved in various synapses of the brain, refereed by the hippocampus and necessitated by protein synthesis. What Rebecca couldn't understand was how places, times, and abstract sensibilities from the past could reappear as if they were as tangible as the present. How could the rich images of her parents' lake house, the aromatic smells of their catch cooking on the grill, and the rhythmic sounds of the lapping water be stashed away as brain cells to be recalled later from the biological hard drive as a carbon copy of the events?

Her brain hurt to think about it.

Suddenly, Alzheimer's seemed that much more natural.

If chemicals and electrical impulses can replay the past as memories on the unaccountable projection screen of our waking conscience, then could it be possible that all of our recorded experiences are nothing more than fabrications of our mind to begin with? Nothing is real except ourselves.

Atom's neurons have been disconnected, marring his ability for recall, which Rebecca deemed unacceptable. She denied that the disease was incurable and that Atom's fate was predestined to failure. New theories were surfacing that a single long-term memory is broken down into various elements and stored in many places at once. If this were true, then Atom's memories had to be somewhere in his brain. They were simply lost along the dendrite super highways in search of receptors.

The dynamic duo was as lost and misguided as Atom's memories. It didn't really matter anyway. She didn't have a specific destination. Trying to track down the memories of an Alzheimer patient was like following a blind tour guide in an art gallery with eyes closed. Rebecca was driving down the complicated synapses of Atom's brain only to find many dead ends and booby traps.

Walter's GPS thought it knew better.

Other than a couple of unscheduled pit stops, Rebecca made up for lost time after being stuck on top of the Ferris wheel for 45 minutes. She was going 80 in a 55. Walter's Audi was much more capable of handling Rebecca's tempo than her own pale green midsize Camry with a brown trim, which was cuddling with Walter in the privacy of his garage.

"Who were the flowers for back there?" Rebecca asked Atom.

She knew the answer already. They weren't for anybody in particular.

Atom took her grave hopping at the Greenwood Cemetery on Park Ridge shortly after the carnival. Rather, the navigation system did. After the GPS offered them the choice of exploration, Atom wanted to visit every single headstone on the property with his newly selected flowers, as if he were in mourning for all. Rebecca had other plans. She swiped the flowers from Atom and laid them to rest at the nearest grave, unconcerned with the identity of the lucky recipient. She then dragged Atom back to the car where their GPS silently planned their next route.

"The flowers," Rebecca continued. "Were you looking for somebody?"

How could he?

Rebecca was hoping they were for her.

"You have reached your destination," the built-in navigation system stoically declared without prior warning.

Rebecca slammed on the brakes. She went from 80 to zero in two seconds. Atom was whiplashed forward to make up for not riding the roller coaster at the amusement park. He relished the moment the best he could.

Again, Rebecca did not understand why she obeyed. The University was still her primary destination, not the circus or a cemetery. She continually allowed herself to become sidetracked from the mission by the retarded GPS. She was to blame.

"What are we doing here?"

Rebecca asked herself the impossible question because Atom couldn't answer and the GPS wouldn't answer. She was speechless, unable to formulate a logical explanation. She checked the navigator's screen to see if its address matched the one on the facing of the office building in question.

They were a match, to her dismay.

"Dr. Linda Grieson...Hypnotherapist."

Why would the GPS take me to a hypnotherapist? she wondered, momentarily suspending reality to accept that the machine had a mind of its own capable of rationalization and judgment. She was losing her own precious mind - her alleged impenetrable piggy bank of memories - that began with her decision to kidnap a 65-year-old defenseless man.

Being a nurse, receiving her degree at the Massachusetts Medical Center, Rebecca didn't accept hypnosis as a legitimate medical procedure, although she admittedly did not know much about the subject. She doubted that someone could be placed in a semi-conscious suggestive state by following an oscillating pocket watch as seen on TV. Even if it were possible, she still had a hard time believing that making someone cluck like a chicken in front of a room full of strangers was no medical procedure. She decided to save herself the embarrassment.

Rebecca was about to pull away when she suddenly remembered reading an article in the *Scientific Journal of Medicine* that discussed hypnotism and its effects on memory loss. How could she have not remembered it before?

Am I supposed to be here?

It made perfect sense.

"Let's go see what Dr. Grieson has to say about your condition," she told Atom, who responded with an involuntary gurgle followed by a mouthful of gibberish. Rebecca recognized her slowly loosening grip on reality as she walked into the office building entitled *1C - Hypnotherapy 2C - Travel Agency.*

"I bet they offer similar services."

Rebecca was disappointed by her first impression. It looked like a normal doctor's office. She was half expecting to walk into a wizardry voodoo worship ground where everything was dark and mysterious. Instead, she got a typical waiting room and a bad case of déjà vu.

"Do you have an appointment?" the receptionist asked.

Rebecca held Atom's hand and scanned her strange environment like a transplanted organism weary of the new habitat. Everything was stained white, right down to the coasters on the table. A fish tank housing three pure white tropical fish abutted against the white wall opposite the white reception desk. Even the background muzak was polluted white. It reminded her of being stuck in an elevator. Maybe she was. White surrounded everything. Dr. Grieson took sterility to an unfashionable level. On the wall nearest the hallway leading to the various examination rooms was a black and white framed photo of a classic 30's style vintage automobile parked on the edge of a cliff, its high beams illuminating the star-filled sky. A television mounted in the corner of the room played the news for patients to occupy their thoughts as they gradually forgot what services they were wasting their money on. Sort of like a pre-hypnosis to the hypnosis. The waiting room even had a proper name, which was displayed above the rim of the entrance door: Patient Decompression Room. However, Rebecca and Atom were the only patients in the room, if they could even be called that. Rebecca wasn't a patient. She was a nurse.

"I'm sorry. I think I'm in the wrong place."

"You're here now. Have a seat. The doctor will see you in a few minutes. Enjoy our magazines."

The Other You; Hypnotic Traveler; Golf Digest.

Atom wandered over to the tank and surveyed the fish swimming in their claustrophobic universe, a relentless connection immediately developed between the two species vying for the superlative of worst span of attention. Just like Atom, the fish weren't complaining about their unfortunate situation. Rebecca knew it would be too difficult to pry him away from his moment. She reluctantly took a seat on the white couch, opting for the news on the television over the recommended reading material, and she waited.

There was no paperwork to fill out. No patient medical history charts to kill time with. *Maybe this place isn't like a real doctor's office.* All she was required to do was live up to the name of the room and decompress for the doctor. That was going to be hard to do, especially after catching the top news story.

"A patient at the South Cove Manor Nursing Home is missing, and his nurse, Rebecca Graffe, seen in this picture, is suspected of kidnapping him. Co-workers offer no motive for such an action, but indicated that Rebecca Graffe seemed unusually attached to this patient."

Rebecca's face turned to match the color of the decor in the room as the news station superimposed her photo over the live feed from the nursing home lobby entrance. To Rebecca's momentary relief, the picture used was an old photo taken when she started out as a nurse, and looked nothing like her. Her face lacked the years of stress and torture, which made for a natural disguise from the past. If the photo wasn't enough evidence, the news station also flashed a police sketch of Rebecca to strengthen their top story. The eyes were slanted and a lot closer together in the subsequent police drawing, her brow furrowed, her nostrils flared. And the shape of her face was much more rounded in the artist's rendering of somebody's inaccurate depiction. They made her out to be a monster.

It was probably Betty, the night nurse, who described me to the police.

That was how all of the nurses pictured Rebecca. Their callous attacks and their warped perceptions were finally to her advantage. But she was still in a lot of trouble. The anchorwoman had a pretty accurate account of Atom.

"...If you have any information about this case, please contact the authorities immediately," the reporter concluded before moving onto a different news story, one much less threatening to Rebecca's livelihood.

Rebecca eyed the receptionist. Luckily, she did not take her head out of her book she was reading to follow the deprecating headlines.

"Miss, the doctor is ready to see you."

They were stuck. All because of the goddamn GPS.

She hoped the hypnotist could dispel the stranglehold on them. That was her only hope.

Dr. Grieson looked like a mother. A good mother. Her voice was toneless, her face was featureless, but there was something comforting about her. An almost unconditional trust was apparent. The perfect facade for her profession.

"Even in a tranquil environment, we are bombarded by sixty thousand stimuli per second," Dr. Grieson pitched to Atom and Rebecca. "The barrage continues every day, unrelentingly. And since the mind operating in its conscious mode can only hold four to seven clusters of information at a time, it falls to the mind in its subconscious to store each and every one of them permanently."

Rebecca was only passively listening to Dr. Grieson. She was struck by all of the clocks in her office, ticking and tocking out of sync, marching to the same beat differently. Time was all around them, a constant reminder of each passing second, never to be recorded or relied upon again. The clocks on the wall were too busy looking ahead to be nostalgic. The hypnotist sat in an executive leather recliner, an oval office knockoff. It reeked of authority and power. Rebecca and Atom shared a brown sofa, separated by a throw pillow named Reason.

"It is in your subconscious where all memories are permanent, and can be recalled whenever needed."

"Even for Atom?"

"I can restore his memories, too. Because the subconscious is the repository of memories and hypnosis is the most direct way of accessing it, hypnotherapy is an effective way to recall information thought to be forgotten. That goes for Alzheimer's patients as well."

Rebecca's eyes lit up with hope.

"We don't cure the deteriorating physical attributes associated with Alzheimer's, but we can reconnect him with his past before he succumbs."

Rebecca was willing to give the doctor, which she still called her in the loosest of terms and in-between imaginary hand-gestured quotation marks, a chance at curing Atom. What did she have to lose? She hoped her skepticism of the whole practice was nothing more than a closed-minded paranoia. She wanted to be proved wrong.

"How are you going to put him under?"

"Biological science," Dr. Grieson responded, as she unveiled a pre-calibrated pendulum from a thin wooden box and dangled it in front of Atom's eyes. "Close your eyes and unlock your subconscious potential."

"He can't follow directions," Rebecca said, no longer impressed or convinced with the great hypnotherapist and her magic pendulum. Her thoughts reverted back to the news broadcast and her defamatory picture plastered all over prime time.

The receptionist is probably on the phone with the cops right now.

The pendulum swung back and forth from Dr. Grieson's fingers. Atom's pupils followed the instrument's cadence as if it were its shadow.

"You're wasting your time."

"Patience. I want you to relax," she told Atom, but directed it to Rebecca.

Just then, Atom closed his eyes, stunning Rebecca's

apparent incertitude of the pendulum and the agent puppeteering it. "Is he under?"

"I want you to travel back with me," Dr. Grieson said to Atom in a most pacifying tone so as not to disturb his fragile state. "You are sleeping on your childhood pillow soaking in all of your past memories back into the conscious mind."

Rebecca never saw Atom so at peace. It was as if he was back on top of the Ferris wheel, stalled in time. She imagined resting her head on her own childhood pillow and anticipated being reunited with moss backed memories preserved like dinosaur fossils in the feathery sediment of her sleepy habitat.

"Electromagnetic waves can affect carbon bonding and cause electrons associated with unstable nuclei to jump to higher energy levels," Atom said like a normal human being with a propensity for chemistry.

For as long as Rebecca nursed Atom at the home, she never once heard him utter anything that wasn't complete gibberish or a direct quote from his favorite movie. She assumed that what he just said was a past scientific breakthrough, even though it sounded like nonsense.

"He's remembering," Rebecca cheered, her white whale of hope finally tamed and baited. "Make him keep talking."

She wondered what was next on Atom's other side of darkness. Would he cluck like a chicken or split the atom? Dr. Grieson continued to dangle the pendulum even though Atom's eyes remained closed.

"The pillow caresses the back of your head. Your brain is saturated. You are once again whole."

Rebecca couldn't wait to disclose her life to Atom all

over again, which was finally coming together like a snug puzzle authored with cement.

"Your father enters to tuck you in while your pillow continues to feed your thoughts," Dr. Grieson invented for Atom's subconscious. "He holds out his hand."

Atom started shifting and convulsing in his seat, his pupils romping around behind his eyelids trying to escape the darkness.

"What's happening?"

"He's having a reaction," Dr. Grieson recited from the book of the obvious. She tried to hold him down, but his involuntary movements were too strong.

"No, Dad, leave me alone!" Atom cried. "Don't cut it. You're hurting me."

Atom ceaselessly kicked his feet in the air as if he were trying to keep someone off him. Short of breath and gagging for air, Atom tried to escape the suffocating terror in his head.

"What did you do to him?" Rebecca screamed, as she watched in horror.

"Help me hold him down."

Rebecca tried to grab hold of his left wrist, but Atom was too spastic to be controlled. He turned his head side to side, his face turning red.

"I'm sorry, Dad," he coughed with the remaining energy he had. "I'm sorry."

What is he sorry about? Rebecca wondered. If this was a sneak preview into Atom's past, then she did not like what she was seeing.

"When I snap my fingers, you will wake up," the hypnotherapist miracle worker pledged, still holding the restless man down. "One...two...three."

As promised, she snapped her fingers.

Atom immediately opened his eyes. His body relaxed and his breathing returned to a state of normalcy. The nurse and the witch doctor let go of Atom.

"Are you okay?" Dr. Grieson asked, after giving him a moment to compose.

"Severed finger soup is better than floating meatballs."

Rebecca balled her eyes out. No hope.

Rebecca wanted no part of Dr. Grieson's witchcraft any longer. The hypnotherapist was more of an instigator to the Alzheimer's than a roadmap to the lost memories. The disgruntled nurse – Atom's caretaker - stood up, only to find an aberration. Underneath her, stained on the couch was a drying puddle of blood. Rebecca placed her hand in-between her legs, just long enough for it to become soaked red with the same substance on the white couch.

"Lions speak in bubbles underneath rabbit holes," Atom explained.

Rebecca watched the blood drip from her fingers.

Severed finger soup.

Rebecca fainted, her head crashing onto the throw pillow named Reason.

CHAPTER ELEVEN

"You have reached your destination."

Norman barely had time to recover from the near death experience on the highway. The destination he and his vacuum were chauffeured to by their GPS was equally unsettling. They were parked in front of a bad memory. For Norman, it was like being at an intuitive outdoor drive-in theater without any hope for closing credits.

It had been years.

"How did you know?" Norman asked his GPS, half expecting it to answer back in its most conciliating tone. It wouldn't be out of character if it did reply. In their young relationship, Norman's traveling companion didn't know when to shut up.

Gloria would have found Norman trapped in one of his cul-de-sacs jutting off the fate line engraved in his hand like a bad tattoo. His boss would have found

Norman out of his sales territory. Instead, Norman found himself in front of his childhood home.

The only way Norman would have come back to 27 Hunter Street was if he was seized by a spontaneous navigation system that withheld secrets. He should have known where he was going halfway through the trip. He didn't. He refused. Even if he wanted to drive down memory lane and reminisce about nonsense, he still probably would have needed a GPS to show him the way.

Not since he was 16 had his feet tarnished this soil. Although much had changed in 30 years, like the green color of the front door and the carport on the west side of the house, its perpetual features were unmistakable. He saw them as drunken ghosts of Christmas past hiding in every corner posing as his personality blueprint. Norman was forcibly thrust back to a time that he schemed to escape as a juvenile delinquent. He vowed never to return. But as easy as it was for him to abscond his simple suburban childhood home and all of the excess baggage it carried inside, which ate away at him like super sized cancer cells, it was comparably easy to be propelled back to reopen wounds. For some reason, it was harder for Norman to leave this time around. He blamed the GPS even though it wasn't forcing him to stay. Its job was done. It brought him to his destination. The rest was up to him.

Norman's eyes were distracted by the tire dangling from the birch in the middle of the lawn like a looped earring. The rubberized sanctuary remained suspended in time from the formative years of his childhood. The tire swing was never used for its intrinsic playful purpose.

He didn't want to be reminded of why he bailed so long ago. The tire couldn't safeguard his world forever. He needed a much larger cocoon to hide away in. Norman thought he was a premature butterfly living in a larvae's stunted body. Anybody else would have suspected the opposite.

Back at the nest, Norman flapped his wings for takeoff, but couldn't get off the ground. There was no breaking away from 27 Hunter Street. Norman glared at his deliverer. The GPS didn't say one word, but the silence was loud and persuasive. It urged him to continue with his journey like a troublemaker hoping to instigate an awkward situation.

Norman opened the door. Reluctantly. The backward traveler wasn't prepared to travel alone. He pulled his unwilling Power Hum Vac 3500X and cautiously approached his only home, expecting his father to greet him at the door clutching a half-empty beer bottle in his drinking hand and his black leather belt in his sanctioned hand. It wasn't necessarily the physical abuse that scared Norman out of town. Major psychological damage was at play, which molded him to become a piss catcher long before he ever promoted the urinal splashguards with the same nickname.

Neurons were firing on all cylinders. Memories were coming back from the dead to haunt their maker, to set the records straight. Norman walked along the driveway that he never dribbled a ball on or backed a car out of. He stood adjacent to the lawn that he never played catch on. The stoop remained sad and lonely for not having a companion to support for the last 40 years. These weren't memories. They were memory placeholders, fillers to occupy what should have been.

The Power Hum Vac 3500X joined Norman for evidence. Documentation of a life not lived. If its job were to pick up dirt and grime, then it would have no problem taking everything in at 27 Hunter Street.

The last image Norman was left with of his father was his hand. It remained outstretched through the doorway, a complex symbol for such a simple message. Like a stop sign, like an impossible impasse, the space in and around his father's five digits did not project a future or dig up an atmosphere of nostalgia. It forced Norman to remain in the moment, the last of its kind for the 16-year-old piss catcher, who thanks to the hand, was forced to leave, never to return again. All of his father's fingers were exercising their authority, singing in unison, erasing a son. The thumb wasn't showing any signs of approval. The index finger was flaunting its authority, commanding a life of banishment and dissent. The middle finger recited its most popular number. Little Norman did not need the ring or pinky finger to spell out his fate for him like a memorable fairytale. His father's hand had always been an unwelcome sight, whether it was implemented to clutch another bottle of beer or to impose brute physical force to compensate for the unattractive lines on its palm, but never had it mimicked the actions of a foot until the day it kicked Norman out of the house.

"What you did to your sister was unforgettable and unforgivable," Norman's father said. Normally, he didn't say anything without having alcohol on his breath, which was for the best, because the natural scent protruding from his mouth was doubly offensive. "I failed. I failed at making you a man. First your mother. Now this. You will never be a man now."

It amazed Norman how his father was a respected sober man in his professional life. A pioneer. He never saw that side of him, unless being a drunken abusive father who talked more to the television set than to his own neglected son was the new parenting method of choice. However, on the day Norman was told to leave for good, alcohol and indolence didn't cloud his father's judgment. He was a professional, for the first time.

"You are no longer welcome here. You never were."

There wasn't a mother's voice of reason to reverse the life sentencing. She died while in labor with Norman. His father never recovered from the enormous blow to the family. The irony was transparent.

This wasn't how Norman chose to remember the events of his childhood. Revisiting the memory at its birthplace screamed for an alternate reality.

"What am I doing here?" Norman asked the vacuum, which didn't respond. It never responded. Norman turned his back on the green door and walked toward his blue Camry while he tried to make sense of the situation.

"You have reached your destination," the GPS sounded from inside the car.

Norman stopped in his tracks, his mind now juggling confusion, fear, and anger. He would only admit to sampling one of the three emotions in the past.

The navigator's audio was louder than usual in its latest command. Her voice had a much sharper tone. Authoritative. Norman remembered the tag line on the box: *The perfect companion for when you don't know where you're going!* The packaging didn't say anything about it being instinctual.

Norman had to choose between the past, with a ghost of his father's hand, and his future, with the discourteous navigation system. He wanted neither, but that would leave him stuck in the present, which wasn't an option that Norman could afford in his fragile psychological state. There was no future. His future was his past. Norman's father yanked him into a past nightmare and the GPS held his head under the water, preventing him from gasping for air's key ingredient: life. They were an unstoppable tag team. If Norman remained stuck in the present, he would explode.

While Norman continued his journey back to the car and his accompanying GPS, he saw a bright red Huffy six-speed bicycle leaning against its kickstand in the street. Was it another ghost from the past or a mental fabrication to ease the harsh realities for a life of excuses?

"Red Lightning."

It was the vehicle Norman conditioned himself to believe helped him escape the abuse when he was 16. Red Lightning was a gift from God. Every birthday and Christmas, he would ask for a bicycle and every year, all he received was disappointment. It was as if his father knew he would leave if given the proper tools. Norman planned his getaway ever since the tire swing on the front yard could no longer provide him with the necessary solace. He scratched and scraped at the walls at nights devising a plan, but he needed a bike to fulfill his destiny.

The circus came to town for the week. As a trapped child, he had always dreamed of leaving home for a life with the traveling circus. He was allured by the concept of being part of the "Greatest Show on Earth," especially after a life on Hunter.

Norman went every day after school to delay coming home. He hoped to be swept away by the traveling circus and living a life with the eight-foot tall gorilla man and the Siamese twins joined at the hip. It would be less of a freak show than staying at Hunter Street. On the first day that the circus arrived, Norman came across a game where the object was to toss a ring around a glass bottle. The prize was a brand new bright red Huffy six-speed two-wheeler. It could be his for 25 cents. He snuck back home and stole a dollar's worth of quarters from his father's secret stash of change in a jar behind his bed.

Each quarter afforded Norman three tosses. He liked his odds because with all of the beer bottles lying around his house, Norman had a lot of practice for this moment. Besides, he had a legitimate desire and will for defeating the game.

A platform supporting dozens of bottles was his game board. The game pieces were three rings glowing fluorescent light. The rules were simple. Participants required a combination of skill and luck. The prize was invaluable. Norman's first toss grazed across the mouthpiece of four or five bottles before settling to rest on the floor.

"One down, two to go, kid," the show runner in the matching red and white pinstriped shirt and hat said loudly. His gaudy sales pitch was working because he attracted a small crowd to his booth.

Toss number two hit the side of a bottle in the first row, knocking it and the surrounding bottles over like a strike in bowling. The crowd oohed and aahed, some whispering that they could do better while others outwardly cheered the unyielding boy on to win the bike. Norman tried to feed off the energy.

"Two down, one to go for a brand new state-of-the-art bike."

He clutched the third and final ring with his hand, picking out his prey. The bottle on the left corner of the platform in the back row spoke to him. That was his target, but with his final attempt, Norman missed every bottle on the platform. A gutter ball.

"Better luck next time, kid. Step right up, ladies and gentlemen. Do you have the skills to win yourself this bike?"

Norman held out the remaining three quarters for the rambunctious circus employee to take, urging him with his desperate countenance to play again. He was playing for his life, a concept the carnie would never understand.

"Seventy-five cents. That's nine tosses," he instructed, handing him nine different colored rings. "Let's see if your luck changes."

Nine tosses later, Norman was forced to walk home. He had four more days to win the bike. He went every day after school, stealing only a dollar from his father's jar each day so as not to be too obvious. By the time he reached the final day the carnival was to be in his town, he had already tossed 48 rings, none of which made it around any of the bottles. He had one more chance to win himself a ticket to freedom. He no longer felt confident.

"You really want this bike?" the carnie asked. "Well, you know the rules."

Norman's local support group surrounded him to

see his final show. They didn't know what was at stake. A stack of rings postured in front of their contestant. Norman's new strategy was to single out one bottle for all 12 turns, but with each toss, he missed by larger margins until he was all out of ammunition.

"Sorry, kid," the carnie said. "Step right up everyone."

It didn't work. The crowd was disappointed. It wasn't meant to be. Norman's eyes watered as he prepared to walk back home with only his pride between his legs.

"Hey, kid."

Norman turned around slowly, embarrassed to have to show his face again, the crowd of disciples still there to offer their support. The sympathetic carnie gently hurled a purple ring at Norman, which he caught with his chest.

"On the house."

"You can do it!" a bystander cheered.

Norman stepped back into the spotlight. Everyone must have known by then that he was playing for something much more valuable than a bicycle. The red Huffy represented his chance at a prize you couldn't win at a carnival. He was playing for freedom. The strategy for his bonus toss was to have no strategy. Overthinking didn't help him before.

He came sidearm and flicked his wrist, as if throwing a Frisbee. The ring spiraled perfectly as it soared over the first three rows of bottles. The congregation of onlookers was silent. To Norman, it appeared as if everything was happening in slow motion. Captivity or freedom? The carnie approximated the ring would land somewhere in the seventh row. Whether it settled to rest as an unexpected champion or as a predictable failure, everyone would have to wait for the resolution of its flight trajectory.

They didn't have to wait too long. Like a swish shot in basketball, the ring landed right through an empty Heineken glass bottle without touching its sides.

The crowd went crazy. The bike was his.

"Congratulations, kid."

Norman was in shock. He never won anything in his life. The carnie presented him with the bike while applause consumed both background audio tracks. He sat on the bike, hoping he remembered how to ride. It didn't matter. He was already riding high. Norman shook hands with a few strangers before pedaling back home.

For the last time.

That night, Norman approached his father's bedside. He was in a deep sleep. The only sound capable of waking him would be a beer can opening. Norman felt obligated to draft a note before leaving home, forever. It was more for his welfare than his father's, who probably wouldn't understand what it said. Without the note, Norman's father wouldn't know he was gone.

Dad – the past is the past. We all make mistakes. We both made mistakes. We both forgot what was best for the family. I am leaving to reclaim my manhood.

He placed the folded piece of paper on the dresser and left without saying a word. Norman had no destination. No plan.

At 16 years old, Norman was without a home.

Thanks to the GPS, he was back. Norman looked back at the street where he previously saw Red Lightning. It wasn't there anymore.

Did he ever see it or was it another failed memory?

Norman started jogging to his car while carrying the vacuum. He didn't want to be in front of his childhood home any longer. He was running back to a place that allowed him to forget. The vacuum suddenly came to life, sucking the air behind Norman as he ran. He pressed the power button, causing the cleaner to scream for mercy. One of the conveniences of the Power Hum Vac 3500X that was an upgrade from the previous 3000X model was that it ran on batteries. No more being tangled up in the power cord while vacuuming the carpet. Was his only friend turning on him, too? It was trying to suction him back in time.

"Excuse me, can I help you?" a female voice shouted over the vacuum's annoying cackle. "What are you doing on my property? Are you lost?"

Norman stopped, still without reaching his automobile, and quieted his vacuum.

"Dad?" he asked, sounding like a whimpering puppy, his back to the newcomer.

"Sir, are you okay?" the strange voice uttered. It was the discourse of 27 Hunter Street. Norman wasn't used to its carol being so conciliatory.

Norman turned around to face his past. Again. He encountered a woman, a pregnant woman, not from his past. She was the new gatekeeper of the memories he thought he deleted. She waddled across the lawn, clutching her stomach, as she neared the lost intruder.

"Excuse me…sir…who are you?" she asked urgently.

"I'm sorry," Norman responded. "I was just leaving."

The owner of 27 Hunter Street weighed the intentions of the intruder against her current need.

"My name is Veronica Maine. Could you please help me?"

"What's the matter?"

"My water has broken and I have no way of getting to the hospital. Could you please give me a lift?"

"Isn't there anyone else who could help you? Where's your husband?"

"I have no husband. I don't have anytime to explain and I don't have anyone I could ask. Would you please help me?"

"I'm sorry, I don't know you, and I don't think I can help."

She was the devil trying to trick Norman deeper into the epicenter of his fears. He barely weathered the storm of memories peppering the outer dimensions of his childhood home. Norman continued walking back to his car, terrified of the GPS' next preprogrammed path.

"What kind of man are you?"

Norman turned around and contemplated her question. His navigation system took him to an ambush.

"Sorry, I was just leaving."

He turned to escape.

"Oh, my God!" Veronica screamed, suddenly heaving in pain.

Norman's heart sunk into his empty stomach. He felt queasy. It didn't go down as easily as the fast food dinners he learned to live off.

"I'm sorry. I have to go."

"You're not going to help me? I'm having a baby!"

Norman ran to his GPS, away from responsibility. He finally made it back to his car, resting the vacuum in the backseat. The navigator stared at Norman from the dashboard as he fastened his seatbelt and ignited the blue Camry to life. The caretaker of Norman's past watched helplessly as Veronica peered helpless at Norman's retreat.

He had to fight the urge to throw a brick through the front window of the house before driving off, shatter the eye of the beholder, but his fear of facing Veronica was too much to bear. Since visiting Gloria for the most revealing palm reading he ever had, Norman, more than ever before, realized how lost he was.

"Where to now?" Norman asked you know who while pulling from the curb and watching his memories shrink in the rearview mirror.

CHAPTER TWELVE

She loved the flowers. Mother Strykowski was right. So was the GPS. HugsNKisses35 placed them in a vase she made in her ceramics class and set it on the kitchen windowsill where the sun's rays would be the most direct on May 20 at 2:32 P.M. The precise day and time of her birth. Jason found her actions to be a dash unusual, even putting aside the fact that her birthday wasn't for another nine months. But then again, Jason had a printout of his family's popularity on Google as a way of courting his date.

Her name was Stephanie Lane. Like a street address. Jason's newest destination. He preferred to refer to her by her online profile name. That was how she was first introduced to him. However, none of the other facts about her floating around in cyberspace seemed to be accurate in person. If TV adds 10 pounds, then the computer must be the perfect weight loss supplement.

Not that she was fat. She did wear her love around her waist though. Despite the four-letter "L" word being too visual for his taste, Jason wasn't complaining because Stephanie wasn't burdened by the inconsistencies in his own dishonest evaluation. She seemed to be interested in both versions of him immediately.

It must have been the flowers.

Stephanie prepared a meal at her apartment for them. It was some form of rigatoni that Jason forced down his digestive track, all the while trying to analyze whether she could be the future Mrs. Strykowski. She was pretty enough, but it wasn't about looks for him. Not anymore. If Stephanie knew Jason's true intentions, she may have doubted her entire astrological formula for matchmaking.

According to her, everyone's fate is written in the stars. Jason didn't know what to say about her quirky belief system. She exposed her superstitions during dinner as if she were reciting concrete facts about the workings of the universe, making the food all the more difficult to swallow.

Jason didn't know how to respond to her when she said words like, "Zodiac" and "Sun Sign." Stephanie was on the offensive early. Jason waited for the opportune time to make his move and take control of the date to satisfy his obligations.

"Jason, are you an Aries?"

"I don't know. I don't follow horoscopes."

"If I had to guess, I'd say...Aries."

Stephanie answered her own question. Jason learned from years of depositions that people already know 90 percent of the answers to the questions they ask. They just needed to confirm their knowledge, or hope to be provided with an alternate reality. Sometimes, he wondered if they were just idiots.

Jason didn't know which category Stephanie fell into yet.

"My reading last week said the planets were aligned for my social life to improve. And my horoscope said it would be wise to seek out an Aries for companionship. I'm a Taurus."

"I had Chinese food last night and my fortune cookie told me that hard work leads to tired feet and rich, fertile soil," Jason wisecracked.

"I don't understand what you mean."

He made up his mind. She was an idiot.

Stephanie believed that all things are somehow connected and that the position of a star 10 million light years away can affect our behavior, and vice versa. Complete lunacy, Jason thought. Almost as bad as taking direction from a navigation system gone haywire.

Jason let Stephanie garble until the well ran dry.

"I know this is a blind date," Stephanie continued, "but our meeting was predestined before we were even born."

"Written in the stars?"

"We're all star stuff."

The conversation lasted the entire dinner. Jason pretended to be interested in what Stephanie had to say while also pretending to like her cooking. He reluctantly convinced himself she would be just as good as anybody else as the mother of his children. He should pursue. Jason had to keep reminding himself his mission wasn't about his happiness. So what if half of his children's genes were hampered by retardation to go along with their genetically deformed love handles from their mother? All that mattered was the act of procreation for the sake of preservation.

"Did the man on the moon teach you how to cook this wonderful meal?" Jason asked with enough sarcasm to last him the rest of the night. "My grandmother was a world-class chef in her day. I can give you her cookbooks."

The first mention of the great Strykowski name rolled off Stephanie's back as if she was a duck. This was going to be a difficult sell.

Jason played the role of a gentleman by helping her wash the dishes in the sink. The flowers enjoyed the waning sunlight through the window, counting down the days until Stephanie's birthday, praying it wouldn't be a cloudy day.

"What should we do now?" Jason anticipated Stephanie would resort to her daily planner for the evening's schedule where she laid out her every move with her unusual interpretations of the slightest renderings in the sky.

All he had to do was make it through the rest of the night without saying too much to incriminate himself, put up with her meaningless meanderings, and maybe he could walk away from the meeting with a down payment for a baby.

Jason didn't need to refer to page 32 of his online family search results, which went into great detail of the Strykowski genealogy from the Wikipedia website, to win her over. He would have to knock the interplanetary particles off their projected paths in order to turn her off. According to her, they were literally a match made in heaven. The gods' version of a twisted experiment in human behavior.

"Let's go for a ride," Stephanie recommended.

"Where do you want to go?"

He was afraid they'd end up on their backs at a barren baseball field staring at themselves in the constellations for the prognostications of their future. It sounded too romantic for his liking.

"If you don't know where you're going, any road will take you there," Stephanie said. "Our destination will be wherever the open road takes us."

She sounded like Jason's navigation system.

"You'll like my ride then. It has a mind of its own."

As the two celestial bodies orbited the car, Stephanie scanned the sky to document the moment. She appeared to be satisfied. Without waiting for a UFO or a shooting star to usher them into the future, Jason and Stephanie climbed inside the vehicle, having nowhere to be.

They sat in silence for several minutes. Jason didn't ignite the car until the forces told him where he was supposed to go. Stephanie, the stars, and the GPS would have to duke it out to be the ultimate backseat driver.

"Where do you see yourself in five years?" Stephanie asked, breaking the vacuum of silence.

"I don't like to think too far ahead into the future. Right now, I'm just preoccupied with salvaging my endangered legacy."

It was all about the future for him. He didn't need his mother to pop her head through the window to remind him of his assignment. Even though Stephanie's question was a bit unfair and presumptuous, it made him wonder.

Where would he be in five years? If it were up to his family, he would be stagnating behind the white bars of a picket fence with his wife and two sons, preparing his offspring to inherit the burdens of being a male Strykowski. If it were up to his job, he would remain fatherless and miserable with no time except the unpromised future, which had stood him up more times than his high school dates.

It was still not determined where the GPS he won from the online dating site wanted him to be in five years. Back at the flower shop in search of a different bouquet for another shot in the dark? Only time would tell.

Stephanie asked him where *he* thought he'd be in five years, not where his mother or his job or his GPS forecasted. He needed the guidance from all three of those factors to pave his path because he didn't know how to rearrange his own stars by himself.

"I'd like to travel," Stephanie said. "Experience the world. I always wanted to see the Swiss Alps. The waterways of Venice."

"Let's go then," he teased. "If we leave now we can get there by November."

Jason turned on the car. To his discontent, the GPS attached to the cigarette holder via its umbilical cord fed off its energy and powered up.

"Those places are in Europe. You can't drive there."

"After one-quarter mile, turn right," the GPS interrupted.

Jason should have expected it, but he was still taken by surprise.

"Well, I guess we'll see about that," Jason said to

Stephanie, who couldn't understand how the navigation system instructed without being programmed.

"How..." she started, but couldn't wrap the rest of her words around the conundrum. Stephanie didn't need to finish her thought. Jason knew what she was driving at. He debated whether he should tell her the flowers were from the GPS.

"It's broken. This piece of junk is just as lost as everything else in the world. It takes me to places I don't want to be."

"After one quarter mile, turn right."

Stephanie smiled.

"Let's follow it."

"What? That doesn't sound like a good idea."

"Come on. What's the worst that can happen? Like you said, we're all in search of something better. Something different. This just may be our chance to start new. Let's see where it takes us."

Jason thought long and hard in silence, trying to find ways to talk himself out of her offer. If he were at work, then he would have come up with a dozen excuses.

"Okay, let's get crazy. I guess we're in for an adventure."

Stephanie clapped her hands. "Into the mystic."

Stephanie didn't know how important she was to Jason's family's future.

Again, not by his own volition, Jason forged ahead, making the desired right turn after the one-quarter mile marker. He had no idea if he was going to be making turns all night or if the mystery destination was just around the corner. Either way, he thought it was the perfect time to make his move and go in for the kill.

"In five years, I hope to be a father," Jason said, borrowing his mother's version of his own future. "Two wonderful boys to help carry my name to the end of days so I'm not just some smudge on the window of time. That's where I hope to be in five years."

"You want children? You couldn't pay me to have kids running around the house making a mess of everything."

Jason's blood froze as he mechanically followed all of the GPS' directions like a drone operated by a disembodied remote control. Stephanie ruined his night. His plans. His future. She was useless.

"Children aren't in your stars?" Jason asked the Sun King, hoping she missed an important star cluster.

"Absolutely not. I hate kids."

"What are we doing then?"

His intentions should have been clearer in his online dating profile. He hoped that her stars would burn out leaving nothing more than an empty black hole of despair. Maybe he could facilitate the process. Put them both out of their misery. There was a telephone pole on the side of the road with his name on it.

"After one hundred feet, you have reached your destination," the navigation system chimed in, disrupting Jason's suicidal thoughts.

The two passengers were silent, curiously awaiting the GPS' destination and its vision for their future. Jason may have been the luckless soul behind the wheel of the car, but he had no control over its governance.

"This is so much fun!" Stephanie shrieked.

Jason slowed to a stop in front of an illuminated directory billboard. He reached his destination, which was an old ironclad one-story building that looked like a military Quonset hut.

Is this another joke? Jason marveled because the sign on the billboard, which referred to the event within the associated edifice, read:

Tonight
Ballroom Dancing
8-10 P.M.

"Dancing, what fun!" Stephanie exclaimed, clapping her hands like the child she never wanted. "Didn't you say on your profile that you were a good dancer?"

He didn't think his lies would come back to haunt him.

"We're going to have such a good time," Stephanie said. "Let's see your moves."

Jason's navigator wanted to expose him as the lying fool he tried to keep from surfacing. He should have known his free device would cause nothing but trouble ever since it brought him to the flower shop. Could this have been his mother's doing still? Flowers and dancing. Somebody was playing a cruel joke on Jason and the punch line was his dreaded four-letter word beginning with the letter L.

"This date is over. I'll take you home now."

Stephanie didn't say a word; her face expressed all of the disappointment she was feeling inside. There was to be no dancing.

There was to be no children.

The date was over and Jason was back to square one.

CHAPTER THIRTEEN

"Show your face!" Norman screamed while knocking over an incense burner and a candleholder in one clean swipe of his overanalyzed right hand.

It used to be so easy to run away from his past. Norman continued to travel ahead in time as his formidable reminders stayed behind where they belonged without any crazy notions of pursuit. Now, his past followed him wherever he went like an unshakable shadow with the gift of an elongated graceful gait. That was how Norman interpreted his unusual circumstance.

Whether he liked it or not, Norman was the perpetrator. He was the one hot in pursuit, hunting down his tragic back-stories one wrong turn at a time.

The GPS showed him the way, reporting each unsought destination as if they were a predictable happenstance.

Not this time around, Norman promised himself, and threatened the GPS, as he sped from his childhood home.

Norman was back at Gloria's palm reading shop. He broke his personal vow never to go back to a palm reader. There were mitigating circumstances that didn't permit him to live up to his word. It was his idea to return, but not for another reading. Norman ignored almost all of the navigator's commands during his route to Gloria's. It once again tried to steer him off-course with the alluring treasures of the unknown and the opportunities for redemption with his past. He was determined to take back control of his life, and that path started with a stopover at Gloria's to show her how much he appreciated her generous gift.

"I know you're here!" Norman yelled. "Come out!"

The establishment wasn't big, certainly not spacious enough to allow for a disassociation with the outside world. If Gloria were at her place of business, then it would only be a matter of time for Norman to uncover her whereabouts like an all-star tagger in a child's game of Hide and Seek. However, if Norman really wanted to find the wonder palm reader, he should have consulted his unflappable GPS. Norman was intent on reaching his destination on his own, a feat he failed to accomplish his entire life. Even Gloria told him that he was an active participant in self-determination, so why was he having such a difficult time writing his desired destiny?

He barreled through the seemingly desolate shop, marking his territory like a tornado on the loose in a town designed by the two oldest porkers in the *Three Little Pigs* fairytale. Norman knocked everything over that wasn't bolted down, the table, the chairs, the purple curtain separating the Reading Room from the Waiting Room.

The place was a mess. Restoring order was a job only suited for the Power Hum Vac 3500X. She would definitely be in the market for one after Norman meddled in her business as she did in his the previous night.

Even the electric sign on the wall welcoming her patrons was torn down as if it was a sarcastic and dishonest salutation unworthy of public display. Gloria was lucky she didn't waste her time putting up all of those superstitious decorations that usually adorn a typical new age outlet, such as the lava lamps and the dream catchers, because they would have been displaced by Norman's uncontested anger. A friend had bought her glow-in-the-dark stickers of the constellations to apply to the Reading Room ceiling to fabricate a certain mood for her clients, but she never had the opportunity to get them up. It was a good thing she didn't. Norman would have plucked each pompous star down from the heavens as they prejudged, computing kismet for the underlings cloaked by their omnipotent forces, until they were all brought back down to earth. Norman was relentless.

Still, the big bad wolf with the nasty palms could not find Gloria. She wasn't in the backroom or the bathroom. She couldn't be found in the closet either.

After an outburst of pillaging, Norman considered she vanished like the rest of his memories, tired of being neglected and abused.

You can't return to the past or at least the same version of the past.

Overwhelmed by exhaustion, he slouched against the wall to regain his breath. He couldn't keep the horrible memories of his father from resurfacing to the forefront of his unmanageable and all-consuming thoughts. Like a rogue wave, Norman was unexpectedly sideswiped again by the disturbing childhood images at Hunter Street and the lifetime of damage they caused.

Norman didn't really know what he would do when he found Gloria. He reached into his jacket pocket and pulled out a black shiny revolver, courtesy of his navigator.

Before he took himself to Gloria's, his electronic companion recommended one pit stop that Norman couldn't resist obliging. It seemed to be the only destination that complemented his plans to get even with Gloria.

He wondered if the GPS was finally on his side.

The gun store had weapons of all shapes and sizes. He wanted something small, quiet, and user-friendly. Something that killed before he pulled the trigger. You'd think someone of Norman's tragic back-story would be adept at handling guns, but he was uneducated in the subject. He couldn't believe how easy it was for him to acquire a gun. The shop owner showed him how to load his weapon and fire before sending him out to the world to have his way with a palm reader who was all-too-honest in her assessments.

Norman slumped to the floor and wept. Cried like a baby. Norman's wrists may have indicated otherwise, but he didn't have it in him to kill. Not anymore. The GPS should have known he wouldn't go through with the murder even in his delicate condition. However, the navigation system didn't want Norman to go back to Gloria's, despite the recommendation to bear arms.

It had a different plan for Norman and his brand new revolver.

He had to leave before anybody came looking for their own answers only to find a crime scene and a madman waving a gun. Norman didn't need to make any more of a mess than he already did. It was time to go.

"Where do I go now?" Norman asked himself, still rocking back and forth on the floor like a boat in rough waters, his cannon perched in his hand ready to fire.

Norman had nowhere to go except away from where he was. He missed his only friend, the Power Hum Vac 3500X. He needed the companionship more than ever. Norman needed help. He was too stubborn to admit he needed the GPS to guide him. He was too stupid to realize the real phenomenon of Gloria's gift.

Think of how the GPS must have felt. It went out of its way to pilot Norman, putting aside its own needs for the benefit of its obstinate master. No gratitude was transferred for the navigator's generous services. All that it reciprocated were bitter complaints and supererogatory name-calling. Norman was blind to his GPS' intent. Sooner than later, his instinctual device would give up trying to help. It would do what any vituperated victim would do and reverse its objective.

Whom was this gun intended for? Norman asked himself again, not really wanting to know the answer. *Most people know the answers to their own questions,* he overheard somebody say at a restaurant years ago.

Norman squeezed the revolver's handle as if it were his world planning to escape through his fingertips. Somewhere between his palm and the revolver's trigger was the explanation of Norman's future.

Suddenly, the bells above the entrance door rang to life, which was followed by the scraping sounds of shuffling feet.

Norman quickly hid the gun in his pants and stood up, scheduling an impromptu meet-and-greet with the intruder.

"Hello, is anybody here?" the enigmatic voice uttered, the mystery man's deep footsteps drawing closer to Norman's hiding spot beyond where the purple curtain once hung from the doorway. "What happened in here?"

Maybe this is whom the gun is for, Norman wondered, almost hoped. At least he now knew it wasn't intended for Gloria. She was safe, for now. He couldn't say the same for himself.

Norman was so close to leaving without being noticed. Now he was stuck at his own crime scene, at least one witness present for questioning. They probably wouldn't need to bring in a forensic investigator to dust for fingerprints. Gloria knew Norman's hands better than anyone else did. He could see the headlines now: Palm Reader Catches Burglar - Recognizes Fingerprints.

"What the fuck did you do?" the visitor asked, as he entered the backroom where Norman failed to hide from view. He now knew firsthand how hard it would have been for Gloria to find a hiding space. Norman was left out in the open, exposed. He searched desperately and fruitlessly to disappear behind anything and nothing.

It was too late. His meeting with destiny came on schedule.

As the man made his way closer to Norman, who remained floored by the overturned table where he had his palms read 24 hours ago, he slowly came into focus for Norman's eyes trying to peek their way through his slanted eyelids.

"Norman, is that you? Goddamn it, it is you. What the fuck?"

"Ralph?" Norman questioned his disbelieving eyes now trying to submerge themselves behind the safety and purblind of his eyelids.

Norman didn't have to see his face to recognize it was Ralph. All he had to notice was his prosthetic arm. Norman was like a rewind button on a VCR that was trying to prefigure the climax of a mystery flick.

What is he doing here?

Norman felt the dead cold chill of his gun in his pants reminding him of its presence. Did the GPS have him purchase the revolver at the gun store for this encounter with Ralph? It would make sense. Norman had been planning Ralph's demise for years.

Norman had not seen Ralph in 30 years. Not since Norman retired from the circus, too tired of the late night travels and the unstable and unsatisfying work parading around the country with America's strangest citizens, which included Ralph, the seven-foot tall rubber band man who could contort his body in ways that made him look like he was turned inside out. Ralph was Norman's favorite freak, or the least intolerable of all the freaks on display at the circus. The 16-year-old Norman never thought he was a member of their misunderstood and disrespected social ranking. However, he was the only one who couldn't find a way to enjoy the wonders of life, which made him the most abnormal of the group.

The thrill of winning Red Lightning was the conduit he used to fulfill his circus life destiny, just as he dreamed it up in the tire swing. Soon after he ran away from home, Norman signed up to be the irresistible loveable kid to introduce all of the freak shows on the playbill in exchange for a meal unworthy of a jailhouse cafeteria and a bed with no mattress or pillows. For two years, he shared a room with the monkey man, one of the carnival's most unusual attractions. He was advertised as being half-ape half-man, and would bounce around his cage for his paying customers, enticing them to throw bananas at his feet. In reality, the monkey man was just a stunted human being with a flattened nose, pointed ears, and hair in peculiar places. The monkey man read and reread *The Art of War* every night before bed. Norman listened to him turn the pages at night, timing the difference between each page ruffle to determine how fast he was reading. It put him to sleep every night. Norman had nightmares of a fleet of monkey men, educated by Sun Tsu's manual of warfare, taking over the world.

The carnie that helped him win Red Lightning took a liking to Norman, becoming somewhat of a father figure to him. He helped Norman find employment. It was the first job he ever had that didn't involve cleaning his father's vomit stains from the carpet. Ironically, Norman would come full circle. He and his dust-busting partner in crime would end up cleaning all types of stains.

Circus life allowed Norman to escape reality and his juvenile past, until Ralph, the human rubber band, forced him into early retirement and into his second career as a crooked salesman to match his crooked personality.

"What are you doing here?" Norman asked Ralph

while getting up from his self-inflicted ruins. The gun shifted about in his pants.

"I should ask you the same question," Ralph responded, studying the disaster consuming the palm reading shop, charging Norman with destruction of private property with his biased eyes. "Looks like a tornado hit this place."

Norman wondered if the GPS knew what awaited him at Gloria's. Should he have listened to his navigation system and followed the directions it provided with the mysterious destination? Maybe he wouldn't have to confront another episode from his appalling past.

Ralph must have felt the same way when he found Norman on the floor. An unexpected surprise. A confrontation to force a rewriting of the past. Not even Ralph, the great contortionist, could twist his way out of this situation.

Ralph was a control freak to go along with being a circus freak. He and Norman would rehearse his introduction for hours before his performance. Ralph would coach Norman's every inflection until the 16 year old would lose his voice. The speech they created together was a real winner that sparked the audience's interest.

"Step right up, step right up," little Norman would sing. "In a world where so many forces are predictable and bounded by their own natural limits, there lives a man that defies all laws of physics."

It would be at this point in the speech where the crowd would start to get anxious. They'd slightly lift the lid containing their excitement with anticipatory shouts and coyote howls. The crowd would erase any nervousness Norman previously had about public speaking and he would finish with confidence and a jolt of adrenaline while Ralph prepared for his moment from behind the curtain.

"In a minute, your eyes will be treated to a surprise they will be questioning for as long as they can see. A man that can stand and sit at the same time. A man that can bend in ways you'd think he has no bones to hold him up. Please give a round of applause to our master contortionist, Ralph Genderson."

The last performance of both Norman and Ralph's carnival careers began like it was their first. The curtain rose. Ralph stepped out onto the stage to a thunderous applause and then executed some simple frame bending exercises as Norman watched the performance from the side of the stage and tried to keep the crowd actively interested in Ralph's contortions. Ralph brought both feet behind his back and over his head, wrapping himself into a small human ball. In that position, Ralph then rolled over and balanced himself on his forehead. After that move, Norman walked back into the middle of the stage and addressed the crowd.

"Ladies and gentlemen, feast your eyes on one of the most difficult positions in the industry. Many acclaimed contortionists have attempted this move only to have it ruin their careers with debilitating injuries. But Ralph is as experienced as he is fearless. Watch as he attempts The Alien Secretion live for the first time tonight."

The crowd was silent. If there were any repeat audience members from the night before, they would have witnessed Ralph perform the very trick that Norman advertised he never attempted. It was all for show and little Norman loved every bit of the drama as if it were one giant escape.

Ralph unfurled himself from the reverse cowbell position and stood up into a normal Homo sapien pose. The monkey man would have vomited. Ralph bowed slightly for the attentive audience to feign gratitude, a less than generous curtsy for someone who could touch his hairline to his toes without bending at the knees. He then slowly contorted into what the instructional books would call The Alien Secretion position. A message of warning to the readers cautioned never to try this move at home unless under a certified professional's supervision.

Ralph, the great contortionist, arched his spine all the way back and around his ass so that his head fit between the backsides of his thighs, all the while, his legs remaining unbent. Ralph appeared to be turned inside out by twisting backward from the pelvis. He did it without breaking a sweat. He then weaved his arms through his legs and around his face and up over his body. This required a temporary dislocation of Ralph's elbows, which he learned how to pop in and out by himself at will.

The crowd went crazy. They felt Ralph's pain, but Ralph didn't allow himself to experience any discomfort. Instead, he taught himself how to submit to an over-relaxed, semi-conscious mental state, leaving behind all of his senses that do battle with life's undesired experiences every day. A self-hypnosis. Ralph tried to coach Norman into reaching such a high level of relaxed consciousness, but he could never get him to let go. The exercise made him even more anxious.

There was always something there to remind him.

The Alien Secretion was always the showstopper and Ralph tried to hold that position for as long as he could to give the audience their money's worth. It was very important for him to remain as still as possible because any extra stress on the joints could seriously injure him. Not once did he ever have an incident beyond a few minor black and blues and sore muscles. He was a professional.

That night though something happened during his final Alien Secretion performance he could not control. Despite Ralph's strong convictions, Norman also had little control over the situation and the unfortunate outcome that ended two careers. Norman was just acting out of unrelenting emotion.

As Norman studied the audience, a hobby he liked to do while Ralph was all tied up in his risky finale onstage, he thought he saw his father in the crowd. It had almost been a year since he escaped from home, or had been kicked out, whichever version he allowed himself to believe, and not once during his time apart from his abusive father did Norman feel like he was being pursued.

"No, leave me alone!" Norman screamed.

Norman did not give himself time to re-evaluate his senses. Reality interfered. He backed away in fear, right into Ralph, who fell over from The Alien Secretion pose, landing on his right arm, which was still dislocated at the elbow and coiled backward between his legs. Ralph winced in pain as his arm snapped by the weight of his body. He was unable to maneuver himself out of position as he rolled back and forth onstage. Norman ran behind the curtain, believing that his past finally caught up with him. A few audience members, including the man

Norman mistakenly thought to be his father, tried to assist Ralph.

"Someone call an ambulance!" somebody screamed out.

Ralph's body quit on him. Even with all of the outside help, he couldn't arch his spine back into a normal position, and therefore, remove his head from between his legs, all the while his arm, which was now turning purple from becoming even more twisted than what is physically possible, was taking the brunt of the fall. Ralph was slipping in and out of consciousness as people from the crowd who didn't know anything about contortionism and how to safely disengage from various positions, tugged and pulled at his fragile extremities.

"Is anybody a doctor?" another person yelled.

The fallen contortionist couldn't wait any longer for help and blacked out.

Norman was nowhere to be found.

The surgeon at the hospital said it was hopeless. There was no way he could save his arm after the major trauma it suffered from the accident. Amputation was necessary.

Norman nervously listened to the white coat's prognosis from the hallway, trying not to feel guilty. Norman wanted to apologize, but was told to keep his distance from Ralph, who would have choked him to death if he had two working hands.

"Not only is his arm broken in three places," the doctor explained to the carnival director concerned more about the bottom of his pants pockets than Ralph's health, "Mr. Genderson destroyed ninety percent of the nerves in his arm beyond repair. If we don't amputate, he'll run the risk of disease. His days as a contortionist are over."

Ralph overheard the doctor's last comment rain down as if it was a career ending injury for a superstar athlete.

"Where is that kid?" Ralph screeched. "I'll kill him!"

Norman feared for his life. Again. Nothing changed from the drudgery of his childhood home where his father reigned with a 12-ounce bottle. He ran down the hospital hall as fast as his little legs could take him, never getting a chance to apologize. Once again, Norman was forced to run away from his life. Once again, he didn't know where he was headed.

Norman and Ralph's paths didn't cross again until Gloria provided them with the appropriate venue for an untimely encounter. Norman couldn't understand why Ralph would go to a palm reader with only one hand, but that was the least of his worries. He had to play his cards very carefully, if at all.

"I've been looking for you for over 20 years," Ralph said, as he slowly approached Norman. "Did you think you could get away with what you did to me? You ruined my career, my reputation, my life."

A serious case of déjà vu overwhelmed the vacuum salesman. Norman pushed himself up to his feet, the gun in his pants trying to escape down his right leg, a reminder of its presence and purpose.

Was the gun intended to be used on Ralph? he asked himself again.

"You ruined my life."

"You ruined mine," Norman shot back. "Why are you here?"

Norman slowly glided along the wall, hoping to reach an exit before Ralph sought retribution for an accident over two decades old. He didn't make the course out of the building any easier with the destruction he caused.

"You're not going anywhere," Ralph promised, as he pulled out a gun from his pants pocket with his only working hand and pointed it at Norman, right between his eyes. It was the exact same revolver as the one making up for Norman's inadequacies in his pants. They were probably display case buddies at the gun store, only separated by a few moments. Norman wondered if Ralph was in the gun store with him. But why would he be? Coincidence? A 20-year planned old-fashioned duel for authority over past events? Norman didn't remember seeing the ex-carnie perusing the firepower Gus offered at his store. Their paths were probably not predestined for an intersection until all of the players and props were securely in place.

Was his gun intended for me? Norman feared.

"Don't make any quick moves."

"You're not my father!" Norman cried.

He was right. Ralph was not Norman's father, which was why the gun was powerless to defend, which was why he would not pull the trigger again. Norman did not like the cards he was dealt. He decided to fold.

"Who brought you here?" Norman asked, almost drawn to tears. He didn't like being the enslaved backward traveler, now wishing he had a home to return to instead of the backseat of his car. "What brought you here?"

Norman didn't want to wait any longer for a response, realizing he would not have any time to reach into his pants for the ultimate comfort of safety. He made his move. He did a quick three step dance past the doorway where the purple curtain used to hang and then he sprinted through the waiting room, out onto the street, and into his car.

Running away from his past again. His GPS was probably doing its best to hold its digital tongue so it would not blurt out an *I told you so* remark and completely dispose of any self-respect Norman had left.

Ralph, on the other hand, fully expected his GPS to remind him he had reached his destination.

Norman wasn't even sure anymore if he could trust his circus memory, wondering if it was all just a façade, the "greatest" escape, to mask and forget the real memories forged on Hunter with his father. He couldn't be sure. He didn't want to be sure.

It didn't matter.

Norman finally knew why his navigation system had him buy the gun. It wasn't to bring down Ralph. There was no question who the weapon was intended for as he quickly drove away from Gloria's palm reading shop… for good.

"After one-quarter mile, turn left."

CHAPTER FOURTEEN

Rebecca was afraid what the hypnotist would have uncovered about her if she were put under by the magic pendulum. Would Rebecca have been reminded of how she was introduced to her final companion, who was infamously known to the world as loneliness? It was ironic how loneliness seemed to be friends with everybody. If only this popular prom queen would bring all of her friends together for one big shindig, nobody would ever feel alone again. Loneliness was a self-serving and undependable friend, an entity that didn't possess the characteristics that went along with her name.

It wasn't hard to see the relationship build throughout the years until they eventually became best friends forever. Inseparable. It started after med school. The signs were obvious that her world was slowly slipping away, but Rebecca's newest friend extended her hand in friendship, promising the riches of never being alone again. Rebecca went from expecting to go out on Fridays, to hoping to go out on Fridays, to brainlessly waiting to be told by her favorite news network that it was 10:00 P.M. on Fridays before being asked where her non-existent children were. Another unnecessary reminder of how alone she really was. Rebecca's inbox also dwindled in size to one or two new messages per day, even though she checked her e-mails three times as often. She looked forward to receiving SPAM, just to feel wanted. Important. Things that Rebecca used to do with others, such as go to the movies, were relegated to participating with her only friend, loneliness, the most popular kid on the block. Rebecca tried to trick herself into believing that she was simply becoming more independent, an inescapable consequence of time. However, she could not help but commiserate over the fortunes of others, and therefore, failed to survive in the moment while in the shallow end of the pool of her own good fortunes. The only respite was her understanding that what she suffered from was a non-discriminating social disease.

Her last visit to the family lake house upstate was with everybody's favorite imaginary friend. It was loneliness' idea to make the trip with Rebecca, her final reluctant return, the first since the life-altering incident 15 years prior. They sat innocently on the dock, dangling their feet in the water, much like Rebecca did with her younger brother every summer with only the greatest of trials and tribulations to worry about, which were not fabricated by years of fraudulent manmade grownup burdens. Over the years, the number of visitors joining Rebecca at the lake house dwindled until it was only her and the lonely escort.

Even with a companion like her new BFF, Rebecca didn't think she could get away with driving up to the lake in the commuter lane. Talking to her crony was also like talking to herself, a lot of fluff with no answers to the pressing questions regarding her lonely situation. Rebecca didn't know why she kept her around, but they were like two peas in a pod. When they were not together, they were not whole.

Loneliness shadowed Rebecca on her shifts at work, too. Every time she thought she found a friend in one of her patients to replace the lonely vagabond tracking her every move, they up and left her for a higher, more unflappable power with promises of eternal paradise. Until she met Atom. He and his Alzheimer's didn't know any better to leave her like everyone else. At first, Atom's disease was Rebecca's blessing. A dear friend not crippled by the pitfalls of friendship. Then she realized that he was no different from the lonesome old fool she couldn't shake from her side.

Rebecca definitely didn't need a hypnotic procedure to remember those days and was glad she wasn't a victim of Dr. Stephanie Grieson's conjuration. She didn't want to be reconciled with those solitary memories. The only way to do so was to save Atom and make him a true friend capable of the shortcomings of friendship. Her newest destination showed little promise for the transformation.

Before she turned any deliberations onto herself, more specifically trying to comprehend the mystery of her bloody leakage at the hypnotist's office, Rebecca exploited all of her heavy thoughts trying to understand why Atom would fear his father's memory to the point of uncontrollable convulsions.

Rebecca's lingering reminders about Atom kept her attention away from the navigation system's directions. She was making the necessary turns with her brain on autopilot, once again failing to question its intent.

Now they found themselves at a psychic medium gathering, courtesy of her GPS. Again, she didn't know what they were doing there. Like hypnotherapy, Rebecca didn't take seriously a profession that communicates with the dead. She may have been wrong about Dr. Stephanie Grieson and her ticking clocks. She decided to give the noted medium, Anthony Stevens, an opportunity to wow her, although she was going in with unflattering prejudgments.

There must not be any sense of design for these uncustomary health care enterprises. Just like the hypnotherapist's office, everything was painted sterile white. Rebecca wondered where all of the supernatural trinkets were. She guessed they wanted to be taken seriously like doctors and psychiatrists. Even the medium was dressed like a businessman on Wall Street, a perfectly trimmed three-piece suit, not in the stereotypical garb you'd see a psychic wear on TV. Rebecca was disappointed. She wished she could have been a part of the entire three-ring circus, which included the colorful costumes to go along with the clowns running the show.

"I'm getting an older male who's also there on the other side," Anthony Stevens said to an overweight mother crying at the round table of paying customers, across from a skeptical Rebecca and an inattentive Atom. "Someone who passed from either lung cancer or emphysema, tuberculosis; it's a problem in the chest area. And I feel like there's a J- or G-sounding name attached to this male figure."

Rebecca wasn't paying attention. The psychic lost her when he started speaking in vague generalizations, taking advantage of vulnerable, gullible participants in search of easing the discomfort of a loss. "Chest area" covers about 50 percent of causes of death in America.

Being a nurse, Rebecca understood the power of persuasion. She knew the entire basis of the psychic profession hinged on the medium's ability to convince his subjects that what he was saying applied directly to their lives, which wasn't hard to do, especially when his subjects would do everything they could to make the psychic's nebulous translations from the hereafter a perfect fit to their incomplete puzzle. It was the perfect ointment, whether or not it was a placebo.

The sad and lonely people at the round table looking for closure were trying so hard to make Anthony Steven's reading from a J- or G-sounding name applicable to them, even if they didn't know anybody who passed with a name beginning with a J or G. They lied to themselves to help their cause.

"My third cousin's husband's niece died from a car crash," the rotund mother said, attempting to win over the psychic's attention for the compassion she so desperately needed. "I think her name was Jessica. Or Gloria. She wouldn't have died unless her heart stopped. That's a chest area death."

Rebecca couldn't believe she allowed Walter's broken built-in GPS to fool her into another ridiculous destination. She would have gotten up and left right then and there if it wouldn't have been such a struggle to get Atom to comply with her hasty audible.

Anthony Stevens was providing a venue for false hope. He was no better than the lying cats on Wall Street.

Rebecca was not impressed. Not yet.

"Wait one second," Mr. Stevens said while circling the table. He held both hands above his head and closed his eyes, concentrating really hard, as if he were listening to someone's conversation three miles away. "Is there an Atom here? I am picking up a strong signal for an Atom."

Rebecca almost fell out of her chair.

Mr. Stevens was specific for the first time all night. He didn't have to play the guessing game by randomly selecting a letter from the alphabet to coax somebody's name to the spotlight. He wanted Atom. Somebody who crossed was looking for Atom through the psychic agent with the abilities to open up the lines of eternal communication. Rebecca tried to remember if they signed an attendance sheet before the performance. She was quite certain everybody at the table was anonymous. Like Stephanie the hypnotherapist, Anthony the medium was redefining the limits of human capabilities and shattering all of Rebecca's presupposed assumptions about the scientific operation of the universe.

"Um, this is him right here," Rebecca said nervously, pointing to Atom sitting by her side, incapable of paying attention to anything. "He's sick and can't communicate."

"A man, possibly a father figure, is coming through and he's showing me yellow flowers," the medium explained, his eyes still closed to keep in touch with the other side of life. "Yellow flowers are usually a symbol for absolution."

What's with the world's obsession for yellow flowers? Rebecca marveled, remembering her navigator's unscheduled trip to the florist before attempting a second, less traditional venue for communication with the dead.

"I'm sorry. I can't help you. I don't know anything about his past to help complete the rest of your fictitious story." Rebecca didn't want the psychic to think she could be exploited like the others. "Tell your dead contact that he's going to have to be a little bit more specific and not talk in obscure mysteries."

Rebecca was still trying to figure out how he guessed Atom's name correctly without the help and input from those at the table. Atom is a common name, even though the only representative present spelled his name differently from all of the others. Anthony Stevens wouldn't know that though. They were all pronounced the same way.

Rebecca also couldn't grasp why dead people didn't just say what was on their minds instead of communicating in cryptic. Why couldn't they just tell the medium what their name was without having to play Hangman? Why couldn't they reach out without the presence of obscure symbols? Anthony Stevens would have told the skeptics that only a few "special" people are fluent in the language of the afterlife. He was one such gifted individual who could translate and project the deceased's messages. Rebecca would have remained skeptical.

She didn't know how to feel anymore.

"I'm still seeing yellow flowers," Mr. Stevens said. "The man presenting them to me for Atom says he is very sorry and hopes he is forgiven."

Rebecca tried to piece everything together. At the hypnotherapist's office, Atom apologized to his father while under Grieson's spell. Now, at the psychic gathering, a dead father figure was apologizing to him. Rebecca was being presented with clues about Atom's past, a past that didn't seem particularly conciliating. She was learning more about Atom now than during teatime back at the nursing home, but she was still far from a breakthrough. Rebecca had hope for her plan.

"Who is apologizing?" Rebecca asked. "Why is he apologizing?"

She was so close. Atom was being presented with flowers from beyond the grave from a dead guy who was overcome with guilt. Rebecca aspired to find out why. Rebecca hoped she could unblock his desolate memory lane and reopen it back up to local traffic. Maybe tourists who once traversed Atom's memory lane would begin to stay for all of the attractions that brought them there to begin with all those years ago. Unfortunately, it was now the central avenue of Atom's ghost town.

"Can you tell me anything else?" Rebecca implored, sensing that she was really close to a breakthrough, which would mean her journey was not in vain.

"He's showing me a scissor. There's blood on the tips. Scissors is usually a symbol of jealousy and distrust. The blood on the scissors indicates something was cut or severed, like a strong bond, an end of a relationship."

"Jealousy…distrust…betrayal!" Atom shouted. "The scissors are real, and so is the blood. All I did was sever the hydrogen bond. Because you couldn't, you had to cut the only tangible threat to your manhood. Now we're even."

"What's going on?" Rebecca yelled.

Anthony the medium opened his eyes. "I lost the connection. It happens every so often when one of the parties becomes too aggressive."

"In the setting moon, we are refrigerator units," Atom said, smiling.

Rebecca sighed out of hopeless desperation. Was her journey destined to fail from the very beginning? Were the nurses right about her all along? Was the GPS nothing more than a broken promise?

"But write this down," Anthony Stevens said. "Because a woman who came through at the end of the read was telling me to say this combination of numbers."

Rebecca armed herself with a pen and a pad. Maybe this would be the answer she was waiting for. Maybe she would be writing the cure to Alzheimer's.

"Seven...two...three...eight...six," the psychic said slowly and methodically.

"What does that mean?"

The fat woman at the table was growing impatient. She was bothered that the psychic was spending all his time on two hopeless cases incapable of being helped. She had legitimate concerns that needed absolute attention ASAP.

Anthony the psychic made another revolution around the table; his eyes remained open to better communicate with the very much alive customers in front of him. The ghostly relatives and loved ones seemed to only get through when he hid his eyes in darkness. They didn't pay him for his services and therefore were not privileged to make eye contact with their host.

"I'm sorry, she's gone," Anthony explained to Rebecca.

She read and reread the unusual code scribbled on her napkin as if it were a magic cryptograph containing the answers to all of her woes. "But the symbols the deceased presented were strong and specific to his longing to apologize. There is somebody who has crossed with an important message for Atom. It's up to you to unlock the memory with this combination."

Rebecca was disappointed. Again. In the end, there was no substantial or meaningful evidence to take away from the psychic other than the nonsensical code that probably had just as much significance as Atom's spastic apologetic rant while unconscious at the hypnotist's office. Her and Atom's entire fugitive journey was all one big tease and the perpetrator was the goddamn GPS getting all of the laughs.

She wanted to leave. Rebecca should have felt fortunate. Nobody recognized them from the earlier newscast. So what if she was taken advantage of by her ex-boyfriend, a hypnotist, and then a psychic? That was still the least of her problems. How could she allow all of these outside factors to steer her off course? She remained determined to win Atom back his God-given natural right of forethought and retention. Rebecca surreptitiously placed the napkin in her pocket and started to help Atom to his feet while the ghost whisperer continued to pace.

"I'm getting another reading. There is a little boy coming through trying to reach out for a name beginning with the letter R." Anthony pressed his fingertips to his temples. "Is there a Rebecca here?"

Rebecca froze in her place.

"He's showing me an injury to the crotch area,"

Anthony read from behind the safety of his eyelids. "Yes, he's definitely reaching out for a Rebecca."

Rebecca remained quiet and frozen, a deer in the headlights of an approaching 50-ton tank crossing enemy territory. For the first time, she wished she were Atom so she wouldn't have to remember. Anthony Stevens was somehow conjuring up a not so favorable recollection from the past, which Rebecca wasn't about to acknowledge for Mr. Stevens, let alone for herself.

"Is there a Rebecca in the house?"

Rebecca tried to act inconspicuous, not wanting to accept the lead role in a scene heading into a depredating flashback. She could see herself turning into the unconscious whimpering Atom from the hypnotist's office if she continued with the charade.

"Don't be shy," Anthony commented, opening his eyes. "Remember, I'm only here to help you. I would never let anything negative come across from the other side."

Anthony scanned the players in the room. There were four women at the table. He wondered which one harbored the lucky name.

The obtuse woman raised her hand. "My name is Rebecca," she lied.

The real Rebecca, the one holding hands with the retarded senior citizen, stood in shock as she watched someone else steal her identity. The elf lady with the pumpkin sized stomach looked more like her from the police sketch than she did.

A good sign, but Rebecca was too distressed to realize all of the outstanding benefits of lending her name to a brave and naive surrogate.

The real Rebecca remained silent. She didn't know what else to do. Her mind was preoccupied with memories she thought she had once forgotten. The fake Rebecca was in for a surprise from her manufactured past she would later regret adopting, wishing she didn't lie about herself.

"I'm seeing yellow flowers again," Mr. Stevens said to the fake Rebecca. "Just like the ones presented to me from the previous reading."

"I don't understand," the fat woman replied.

The real Rebecca understood completely. She was trying to force amnesia onto herself so the last 20 minutes became an unexplored blip on the radar. If Rebecca wanted flowers, she would have kept Atom's for herself.

"The yellow flowers mean absolution for you, too," the medium continued. "There is someone on the other side who is trying to apologize. He wants me to tell you it isn't your fault and you shouldn't continue to punish yourself by not living your life to the fullest potential. I don't know what this means, but I'm being told you can hang up your clothes again."

Rebecca, the real Rebecca, heard enough. It was time to go. She grabbed Atom and helped him help her escape from the table. Rebecca hoped to leave the burdens associated with the deceased party poking around the land of the living at the table along with her name. She should have never come to begin with. Everyone phony. Even herself. She was not immune to the flawed characteristic.

"I have to go," the real Rebecca told Mr. Stevens, as she guided Atom toward the door. "I'm going to get a head start on interpreting this message."

Whether her statement was true or not, she still wanted to get the hell out of there before anything else was revealed. The fake Rebecca preoccupied the medium with questions about a life she never lived while crying, preventing him from convincing the real Rebecca to stay and listen to others get more out of her own life than she would ever obtain from years of actual firsthand experience.

"I had an uncle who was born with one testicle," the fake Rebecca lied.

The real Rebecca had reached her tolerance level. She grabbed Atom by the arm and walked him briskly out the door, cursing a world built on deception.

CHAPTER FIFTEEN

Jason couldn't believe he was having drinks with a total stranger who referred to himself as Aces, the master pickup artist.

After dropping his blind date off from a night of not dancing and not making little baby Strykowskis, Jason allowed his prizewinning GPS to dictate the rest of his night. The navigator already bought him flowers and directed him to a ballroom to partake in his favorite social activity, which would have made his one-legged grandmother proud. It might have been the best date he had ever had. Why not see where it wanted to go next? Stephanie Lane was as useless to him and his family as a genetic disorder.

The navigator's next desired destination was a small colonial-style brick building in a town three exits further east down I-35. Luckily, the navigation system displayed the address of the desired destination on its screen; otherwise, he wouldn't know which apartment to ring. Jason couldn't understand why he was following through with the commands. The GPS had him hypnotized by the allure of the unknown. It was more than an overwhelming sense of curiosity and boredom he pursued. It was almost as if he was coerced into following, with no other destinations to explore. Not even the old stomping grounds could attract him.

Jason was buzzed up to apartment number 3H where he met Aces, an unimpressive man sprawled out on a couch, wearing only boxers and potato chip crumbs, while captivated by a late night infomercial.

"It's all done by computers now," Aces said, Jason's maiden introduction to the self-proclaimed master. "Isn't it amazing? Puts my vacuum to shame."

The infomercial advertised a small circular cleaning device that drove itself around a carpet, without human intervention, finding the hardest to reach places on its own like a robotic cleaning lady with a built-in memory.

"Utilizing laser senses, the Razor M7500 Robot Dust Crawler will go places that no other vacuum cleaner has ever gone before," the infomercial salesman pitched in a gaudy cartoonish voice. "The Dust Crawler can be programmed to memorize the configurations of twelve different rooms, allowing you, the owner, to take a vacation while it cleans your entire house. And if you call now, this technological wonder can be yours for three easy payments of $44.95."

"I've seen it all," Aces commented. "This Dust Crawler will put a lot of people out on the streets. Whatever happened to a mop and a bucket of water?"

"Excuse me, who are you?" Jason asked, as he neared the stranger and his hairy gut with more food on it than in it.

"Do you want the deluxe package for three hundred dollars, which includes three consecutive weekend nights out with me, or just the two hour free trial?"

Aces had his own sales pitch rehearsed, but didn't perform it as enthusiastically as the professional on the infomercial.

"Hey, I'm not that kind of guy. I need to be wined and dined first."

"Relax. Didn't you see the ad? You get laid or you get paid. It don't get no better than that, does it?"

"I don't understand. Who are you?"

"Come on. Let's go for the free trial. You look like you could use a little help. You want me to drive?"

"If I drive, we may never get to where we want to go."

Aces opened up his garage and unveiled a mint 1964 red Corvette with a license plate displaying the name of his alias.

"Are you some sort of shrink or something?" Jason asked.

"You could say that."

Jason was so confused, but like with his navigation system, he didn't ask any questions; he just let himself be taken away. Aces could have been a serial killer.

He wasn't.

As they traversed together, Jason learned the extent of his services in much greater detail, Aces guaranteeing he could help him get any girl he wanted.

Jason was preoccupied with trying to figure out

whether his GPS was like the intuitive robot vacuum or if he was in possession of something much more powerful.

"It's not about looks for them," Aces explained while taking Jason on a mysterious wild goose chase. "It's not about anything for them. It's about what you want and how to get it. You have to approach women as you would approach a car salesman. You have to be the one in control of the negotiation for the merchandise. Do you understand, my friend? This is invaluable advice I am imparting for free."

Jason nodded. He didn't understand. Aces didn't give him time to digest his harangue, suffering major diarrhea of the mouth.

"I'll help you close the deal. You will get laid tonight."

It wasn't about sex for Jason. His investigation for a woman was strictly biological. He wouldn't know how that explanation would go over with Aces, so he remained quietly attentive to the master's lecture as he drove.

"It's all a game. And there are winners and losers." Aces must have rehearsed this a billion times into his rearview mirror. "I will teach you to be a winner."

Jason was intrigued. Maybe he could help convince some girl to mother his future son to Strykowski greatness. His GPS did it again.

"You need to come up with a codename for yourself. You know why I'm Aces? Because I can be both high and low, my friend."

"A codename? I don't know. What's wrong with being Jason Strykowski?"

"Jason Strykowski? That's boring. Come on, we can do better than that."

Aces obviously didn't know about the great Strykowski

history that was dying with each non-reproductive day. Where were Jason's Google search results when he needed them?

"You need a codename. That's rule number one. Do you want to close the deal? Just trust me on this one. I know what I'm talking about."

"Action Jackson."

Aces shook his gut with laughter. "Action Jackson," he repeated. "I like it. All right, AJ, tonight, Aces is your wingman. Relax and enjoy the ride."

They went to The Water Wheel, a small dive bar 10 minutes from Aces' apartment consumed in dimness and white noise. It smelled of urine and vomit. A vacant pool table with only the striped balls scattered haphazardly about the green felt surface was situated by the window next to the jukebox hungry for quarters. Across from the bar, past the carpeted floor supporting small circular dinner tables was a caddy-cornered small platform on top of which stood a microphone for karaoke from earlier in the night. It stood underneath a TV monitor displaying Quick Draw.

Aces and AJ found two barstools nearest the entrance. They parked themselves in front of the bartender, ordered two beers, and surveyed the land. Like a predictable happenstance, three women sat across from them. Not even the GPS could have set a more perfect scene to comply with Aces' plans.

As Jason stared at the attractive herd of Y Chromosomes laughing and having a good time across the way, he received his first free lesson of the night from Aces.

"It's not an insult. Think of it as a backhanded compliment. Trust me. Women don't like nice guys."

"What should I say? I'm not good at this."

"Pick out the girl you want to get with and ignore her. Don't even give her the time of day. Engage one of her friends instead. Ask a question you already know the answer to. When you get your response, quickly turn your attention to your intended target and give her a neg. She'll be yours faster than an express train on a local track. That's Aces' guarantee."

"What the hell is a neg?"

"You never heard the expression 'neg?' Don't worry; my method doesn't require a high IQ. Just recite what we went over in the car. You'll be fine."

The GPS was evil. Jason was certain he fell victim to some sort of voodoo spell when he accepted his online prize. He wanted to be back home in front of his computer desktop screen. He wanted to be where he felt most comfortable. Back in his element. But all of those places were burned in the fire of his dissipating past. The three girls were his future. Jason could find no detours saving him from his destiny.

"I'm doing this for the Strykowski name," he mumbled.

Jason was so nervous as he stood up from his barstool. Never would he approach a group of strangers of the opposite sex in the past. He walked over simulating confidence in himself and recited the adopted neg Aces offered in the car.

The girls were too absorbed in chatty conversation to recognize AJ's approach. Jason singled out the dark-haired girl sitting in-between the two blondes as his target for carrying his son and the future of the Strykowski name into the future. She was the most attractive, but that didn't matter. Not for Jason. He went with the brunette to satisfy his wingman's ego.

It was time to make Aces and his mother proud.

"Ladies, I was wondering if you could help me settle a little bet I have with my friend over there," AJ said to the least attractive girl of the group while pointing at Aces on the other end of the bar. Jason consciously refused to make eye contact with the dark-haired beauty in the middle.

Jason's voice was wavering nervously. He wasn't living up to his nickname. If this were any other night, if his GPS didn't take him to Aces' apartment, he would have never approached a group of women at a bar. Jason was already ahead of his own game. Now Jason wished he still had his printout of Strykowski Google results to seal the deal. He had his favorite sections highlighted.

"What would you say is the color of my shirt?" Jason posed, trying not to sound too queer with his inquiry. He should have come up with a better question, but Jason was not used to thinking on his feet and Aces guaranteed success.

The group giggled as they silently judged the stranger, using their sixth sense to inspect and dissect. Jason hoped they were going to reel him in, but first, he had to bait his hook. He remembered Aces' warning before the sociological experiment to transition into his pre-calculated neg as quickly as possible. Jason wasn't looking forward to that derogatory step in matchmaking. It was integral. The entire scheme could crumble without the playful insult.

"I'd ask you, but I can tell you aren't the brains of the group," Jason worked up the courage to say to his target, which Aces assured was not an insult.

Jason turned his back on the girls and walked back to

Aces, exactly how he was coached to close the scene. He was skeptical.

How was his insulting behavior going to woo the chirping birds perched across the bar flapping their wings for compliments? He wouldn't want to co-parent the child of someone so offensive, but it *was* Aces' guarantee. He was a professional swinger. If Aces heard the question that Jason came up with for the girls, then maybe he would have retracted his pledge to stand by the assurances of his services.

"Well done," Aces complimented. "Five minutes and she's yours."

"What was the nickname for?" Jason asked, sitting back down, eyeing the girl he just negged, wanting so badly to go back over and apologize.

"Gives you a chance to be someone else for a change."

Aces and AJ drank. And waited. Five minutes didn't even expire for AJ to get his money's worth. Imagine what could be done in the three-weekend night package.

As if right out of Aces' guidebook to getting laid, the dark-haired girl approached AJ and his personal assistant accompanied by one of her blonde compatriots. Jason was stunned, unable to comprehend why she would pursue after what he said.

"My name is Sheryl," Jason's target said, smiling and giggling, her chest heaving with excitement. "This is Christine. Come sit with us. We were just talking about how the blue in your shirt matches your eyes perfectly."

Jason didn't know how to respond. Aces would have taught him a second neg if Jason bought the deluxe package. He didn't.

The girls walked back to their perch, mesmerizing Jason with their derrières.

Aces lived up to his promise. His job was done.

"Well done, my friend," Aces said. "Go get 'em, AJ."

"You're leaving?"

"Call me when it's over, unless you go back to her place. In that case, call me in the morning. I like to hear all of my success stories."

"Any advice?" Jason asked the master before he was left to fend for himself.

"You are not Jason Strykowski tonight. You are Action Jackson."

The girls were waiting. Jason approached again, cautiously. Alone. No Aces. No Google. No more pre-constructed negs. His last few encounters with women this unequipped didn't turn out too favorable. Speed dating and online dating were failed experiments testing the variables of his future.

Jason couldn't handle another rejection.

He sat farthest from his target, in-between the two blondes. He ordered three drinks, one for him and the two blondes, purposely forgetting to accommodate the dark-haired beauty; exactly how Aces coached him.

"Aren't you forgetting somebody?"

"Sorry, I didn't know you still wanted to drink. Thought you might have had one too many already. My mistake."

Jason's second attempt at a neg would have made Aces proud. Not only did he come up with it on his own, it rolled off his tongue without the slightest hesitation, like a seasoned veteran. The blondes were rolling. The brunette didn't know how to react, but Jason was grateful because her friends were doing his dirty work for him by getting the brunette to relax and take the neg in stride.

Aces was a genius. He was in. There was nothing he could say or do to ruin his chances. He pictured his mother, holding her grandson, her twin grandsons, the future of the Strykowski name never brighter.

"What's your name again?" the target asked, showing interest.

"Action Jac...I mean Jason. Jason Strykowski."

"No way," she said, a look of amazement enveloping her countenance. "Is this a joke or something?"

The three girls giggled.

"A joke? No, that's my name. Jason Strykowski. What's so funny?"

"That's my name, too. Strykowski. Sheryl Strykowski."

He didn't remember reading about a Sheryl Strykowski in his stack of Internet search findings, fearing his date was turning into a long lost cousin. How pathetic.

"Hey, maybe we're related," Sheryl proposed, the two other girls unable to control their giggles in reaction to the strange coincidence.

Maybe they were. Maybe they weren't. Jason had a passing vision of ushering a 100 percent purebred male Strykowski into the world. He would be the king of the family. His mother would never question his priorities again.

"You two must be related," one of the blondes said, destroying any fleeting hope Jason had of walking away with a chance for a son. "I bet you share distant relatives, like great-great-great grandfathers or something."

"I almost asked for your number," Sheryl said. "That would have been weird. Imagine trying to explain the wedding invitations to people, trying to convince the neighbors we aren't brother and sister."

The girls laughed. Jason followed, but there was no truth to his relief. He was defeated. Again. He knew the date was over. The two Strykowskis would never mate, even if taking a blood test on their first date confirmed their irrelativeness.

The perfectly crafted neg was for naught. There would always be that feeling of being on a date with your sister. The GPS had a perfect record against him.

"You don't happen to have any brothers or male cousins who plan on having children?" Jason asked, hoping for another male Strykowski willing to accept his mission, which Jason was rapidly realizing he had no qualifications taking on.

"I don't understand. No, I don't have a brother. Do you have an Uncle Frank?"

Jason finished his drink and politely escaped.

He longed to be home.

Home was where he was headed, no matter what or who suggested otherwise. It was time for Jason to regain control of his life. He waddled about in night's darkness, feeling like more of an idiot than when he failed at the whole speed-dating thing. The first order of business was to find the nearest receptacle to deposit his dubious navigation system.

He had to make the embarrassing call to Aces. He needed a ride back to his car. The game was over. He forfeited. For good.

CHAPTER SIXTEEN

Norman named her Pamela.

They had been driving together for two days. It was about time they got to know each other on a first name basis. The vacuum in the backseat of Norman's car was overcome with jealousy seeing his best friend cheat on him. Norman did everything she said. Turn for turn. And it was making the Power Hum Vac 3500X feel unwanted. It longed to dance one more time with his favorite salesman. Unlike with Pamela, the smart-talking GPS, Mr. Hum Vac always let Norman lead.

There was another friend of Norman's in the car that was getting more attention that the old time dirt-sucking compatriot neglected by the neglected.

The gun. It rested in the glove compartment, wanting to be reunited with Norman's palms as if it were an obnoxious, know-it-all palm reader. As if it were Gloria. However, until the magnum became a judgmental conniving bitch, Norman would continue to coddle its handle for affection.

Norman and Pamela had a love/hate relationship. He despised her for all of the places she took him to, but at the same time, was grateful for the adventure. Pamela had mixed emotions for Norman. She seemed to be making an alliance with the magnum trapped in the glove compartment. Freedom in exchange for helping to bring down their owner, one wrong turn at a time.

"After one-quarter mile, turn left," Pamela uttered.

Norman wondered what was hiding for him around that left turn. Would he be reunited with the piss catchers at the bar for their redemption?

"Where are you taking me?"

She didn't respond. They were playing games again. The vacuum in the backseat loved every minute of their newlywed dispute.

"I'm not going to make the turn unless you tell me what's there," Norman barked, as he continued to drive, approaching the one-quarter mile mark.

"Turn left now."

Norman slowed to a stop at the intersection and peered to his left. The name of the desired road was 'Memory Lane.' Norman didn't have the privilege of relishing in the cleverness of the name. What immediately caught his attention was the sign introducing him to his left turn.

DO NOT ENTER
ONE-WAY STREET

"Turn left now," the navigator said again, almost challenging him to make the illegal turn. The road was wide enough for only one car to travel and it stretched for an unforeseen distance, curving around many bends, twisting around storefronts and restaurants abutting against its sidewalk. The end, Norman's potential destination, which dissolved into a vanishing point along the hazy horizon, was nowhere in sight. Another mystery trip. Another potential disaster.

From what he could gather in his limited point of view, there were no cars driving down the road toward him. Not even the loyal vacuum could suction him back to reality.

"Turn left now."

Norman inched his vehicle forward for a better view, the nose of the car poking past the Do Not Enter road sign, unable to believe he was even considering making the turn. There was no reason to ever trust Pamela's sense of direction. After doing battle with the one armed contortionist, Norman should have known better. Her voice had a hypnotic tone though that seduced him into naughty things.

"Turn left now."

She was relentless. Pamela was only a preprogrammed computerized voice, but Norman could have sworn she was gaining a persuasive personality the more Norman tried to ignore her commands.

He had no alternatives. Going in through the out door made more sense the less he thought about it. Dangerous, yes, but safer than running into another memory of his abusive father. He was up for the challenge.

"You better know what you're doing," Norman told Pamela, as he pressed slightly on the accelerator to nudge his car down a desolate Memory Lane. Nobody was around to offer any support. As he passed a closed down gas station, Norman thought he saw life in the shadows, but he remembered that his life, which would be the only entity present to cheer him on, had no light to make any shadows come alive. The ignited streetlamps were Norman's only public following.

Norman drove down the road slowly. His mind was racing to make up for the lack of speed in the car. He kept his eyes peeled for oncoming traffic. It appeared that nobody had graced the town with their presence in years. He was in an unfamiliar part of town, even to the locals, but for some reason, Norman felt like he had driven this way a million times in the past. Most of the stores he passed were out of business and boarded up. The garbage cans on the sidewalk were empty as if they haven't been fed in years. Norman imagined he drove himself right into an apocalyptic video game. He was experiencing the fall out.

A cigar shop, a liquor store, and a nursing home roped off with police tape were the only places that Norman could make out clearly at 14 miles per hour. The other buildings must have been low rent apartments or hangouts for the Ebola.

"I think I found a new home for you, buddy," Norman said to his vacuum cleaner, which probably would have welcomed the change in scenery.

Suddenly, two bright headlights burned through Norman's dirty windshield, growing bigger and stronger by the second. His entire life flashed before his eyes, which was not a very pleasurable experience based upon how regrettable his life had been up to that point. The headlights from the oncoming car finally provided the brightness to create the appropriate shadows for him to hide behind. Everything was now illuminated. He never saw so clearly in all of his years. A revelation of epic proportions. Pamela knew all along.

She wanted him dead.

The approaching car with Norman's life underneath its brake pedal sounded its horn loudly, which in the English language would have translated into, "What the fuck? You're driving in the wrong direction." How could Norman be going the wrong way? His navigation system, which was the perfect companion for when you didn't know where you were going, told him to enter the narrow passageway. Norman didn't know whether it was the catapulting bright lights playing tricks with his mind or the sudden realization of his destiny, but the blinding headlights started to look like the scars on his wrists and the barrel of his newly purchased magnum. They all had the same intentions and were trying to convince Norman to succumb. However, as he had always been in the past, Norman was obstinate. He was nauseous from the constant reminders in the headlights, so he screamed and slammed both of his feet on the brake pedal while swerving out of the way from the car playing chicken with him, crashing into a neglected newsstand happy to make the news.

The opposing car was no longer in sight, but the Doppler effect of the horn was still making its fading presence known, still yelling out, "Fuck you!" Before Norman swerved to avoid the collision, he was rewarded with a clear view of his dueling driver, the benefactor of his demise. He saw himself, no different from the near collision on I-35 earlier that day. As the two cars crossed paths, everything slowed down, and for both participating actors, curiosity replaced their sense of terror. Both rubbernecked the other. The man behind the wheel of the car also appeared to be frightened well before he met Norman head on, but what really surprised Norman was the man's version of Pamela suctioned to his windshield, probably predicting everything that was and wasn't meant to be.

Poor bastard, Norman remembered thinking.

Norman also felt vindicated in the whites of the other driver's eyes. He, too, must have noticed Norman's Pamela nesting like a parasite on the windshield infecting the host with powerful and irresistible suggestions. Even though he was in the wrong, traveling down a one-way road the wrong way, Norman felt like he had been forgiven because they shared the same technological disease. In a sick and morbid way, Norman almost wanted to hit the other car. In doing so, maybe they could have helped each other out or at least commiserate together. Their predestined meeting was the closest Norman had been to another who he could relate to in years.

"That was a close call," Norman said to himself, as he regained his composure after crashing into the newsstand, making headline news.

"After two hundred feet, turn left," Pamela said.

The crash didn't faze her. She had places to go. People to see.

Norman wasn't injured, physically. The Camry was. It took Norman a few tries to resuscitate it back to life. He shifted his damaged vehicle back onto the road and tried to will his dying automobile the 200 feet. It sputtered and coughed the entire way, its engine not cooperating with its small, red, triangular shadow displayed on Pamela's revealing epidermis, which was advancing smoothly down the map. Norman tried to push his car forward, but the acceleration was too much for the hunk of metal to handle. As they made their left turn together, the Camry slowed to a stop and died directly on top of railroad tracks.

"You have reached your destination."

Norman was surrounded by nothing except for the tracks underneath him, which seemed to stretch to eternity in both directions. The dormant crossing gates stood guard on either side of Norman's car. Waiting.

"This is just great," he said, pounding his palms on the steering wheel. He fumbled for the keys, raping the ignition's keyhole, and tried to assist them in turning the car on. Norman pushed and twisted and turned, but he could not force even a mechanical response.

"Come on, come on."

The car grunted and moaned, but it was all one big tease. Norman slammed against the wheel again and glared at Pamela. He pulled the car keys out of the ignition and squeezed them in his hand in frustration.

"You have reached your destination."

"You stupid shit, my car broke down in the middle of nowhere. This is not my destination. Do you hear me?"

She didn't respond. Pamela didn't like being talked to that way. Every time Norman yelled at her, she hibernated into silent mode.

Silence.

Norman caught his vacuum mired in disappointment through the rearview mirror. This would have been a good time for him to have a cell phone. Again, his utter disregard for people led him astray.

A really low car horn sounded in the distance.

Hope, as long as it wasn't the same car horn from the variable involved in the near collision in the alley. Norman honked his horn back.

It didn't take long for Norman to receive a response to his honk. They were talking in Morse code. The other car's horn was getting louder, but was still a good distance away according to the spatial interpolation in Norman's sense of hearing.

Something wasn't right. The ground underneath him began to shake.

"You have reached your destination."

Norman looked up nervously. What he saw was no automobile offering the assistance he needed. Instead, he found himself face-to-face with a train chugging down the tracks straight toward his stationary position that couldn't be amended. Pamela knew exactly what she was doing. She was a cold-hearted murderer. The crossing gates descended and blinked red in caution, trapping Norman within the grasps of their tentacles. It was no car horn that Norman was hearing. It was the sound of a train's whistle gawking for his death.

A plume of smoke rose from the train as it snaked nearer, the first cart coming into focus, the headlights putting the oncoming car's brights from the alley to shame. The earth quaked underneath the car. The vacuum shook in fear.

Norman became frantic. After several failed attempts at insertion, he finally forced the key back into the ignition and twisted his wrist back and forth hoping to will his vehicle off the tracks. The train screamed louder as it drew closer; Norman sensed the space between his life and death was 500 feet and closing fast.

Pamela's screen displayed a story that was inspired by true events. The triangular icon representing Norman's car sitting atop her artistic rendering of train tracks was pictured exactly like the real life circumstances surrounding her, but she could not express the danger in the scene to any degree of accuracy.

"You knew this was coming!" Norman screamed at her, wishing he collided with the car so he wouldn't have to deal with the monster barreling down on him. At least he would be able to watch his death as it happened in Pamela's window.

"Make it stop!" he shrieked.

The key and the keyhole were not exciting themselves to an orgasmic epiphany. The car coughed weakly. The engine revved slightly. No combustion resulted. Norman's life rested in his wrists as he continued to twist those keys.

Gloria wasn't looking in the right places. If he dug a little deeper with his rusty razor blades, maybe then he could have discovered where his life was hiding.

Three hundred feet.

It was decision-making time. Could he abandon his car, along with everything inside, for his safety off the tracks? Did he have time to rescue Pamela, too? He wondered. He hoped.

The vacuum had no chance.

Norman reached for the door and pushed, but it would not let him out. The doors were stuck in a locked position. He towed the handle and kicked at the glass window. Nothing. He was trapped.

Two hundred feet.

The train screamed for Norman to reconsider. What may have appeared to be a suicide attempt to the conductor operating the freights was anything but. Norman didn't want to die. He was being murdered. And the killer thought of everything to make it look like a suicide. Although Norman wouldn't make a strong case for himself at the autopsy with the two scars on his wrists and the gun in the glove compartment.

"The gun!" Norman exclaimed.

He almost forgot all about the gun. Now he understood why the navigation system had him purchase it at Gus'. To put him out of his misery.

Norman rifled through the glove compartment and pulled out the already loaded magnum. He could have settled for the standard pistol at the gun store, it was almost $50 cheaper, but at the time, Norman wasn't thinking so rationally. As the locomotive carried Norman's death certificate, his head was finally clear, which would make the bullet entry wound seamless.

One hundred feet.

He held the gun up to his temple with one hand while trying one last time to start the car with his other. Both extremities were shaking, making his ambidextrous attempt near impossible. The keys of life rested in the palm of his left hand while the instrument of death existed in the palm of his right.

"You are at a crossroads in your life," he remembered Gloria the palm reader tell him, "and you will be forced to choose a path to your future."

"Shoot the window, idiot," the vacuum cried out but could not be heard.

Norman's face burned red as his vehicle's engine continued to fail. The car may not start, but his gun definitely would.

"The window," the vacuum tried one last time. "Shoot the window."

Fifty feet.

The train was close enough for Norman to see the conductor's face. He forgot that there was a person in charge of that machine. Until then, Norman saw the train as a mechanical monster. Same as he viewed Pamela. The conductor's face was equally terrified as he tried to wave Norman off the tracks; the whistle that once sounded like a distant car horn now reminded him of an earth-shattering explosion.

There was little time. Norman decided to give his car one more chance at starting up. If not, he'd have to make his ultimate decision. The train or the gun. Which medium would he select to satisfy the GPS' final destination?

Norman violently twisted the key in the ignition and screamed to match the decibels of the approaching train's whistle.

CHAPTER SEVENTEEN

Sergeant Victor Riley required both of his ears, as well as his disproportioned nose in order to see clearly. His thick, black, horn-rimmed glasses made him appear a lot smarter than he really was, but intelligence wasn't a trait that he had ever had an interest in pursuing. Even at the age of 32, Victor couldn't name the 50 nifty United States, always forgetting to mention the Dakotas and New Mexico. The latter state he thought to be a country in Europe, north of the original Mexico where the locals rode donkeys to taco stands and spoke the Mexican language fluently. His former partner bought him a cheap GPS as a joke so that he would know that New England wasn't in South America with its mother country. Up until a few weeks ago, Victor was also ignorant to many of the skills necessary for making a successful law enforcer. There were times when Victor was reluctant to arrest a criminal because he knew he would forget the words to the Miranda rights. Despite his immunity to learning, Victor still managed to be promoted from officer to sergeant.

He was beginning to think that it might never happen. Five years on the force and not once was he considered for a career advancement. Most of the other officers in his class were moving up the ranks of distinction, some even becoming lieutenant or detective, displaying twice the amount of medals on their uniforms than was displayed on his scarcely decorated outfit, which was probably overdue for a date with his complicated washer machine. Recently, out of pity and part of a mean-spirited joke, Sergeant Riley received a small pin for bravery for breaking up a bar fight between two drunk mothers, but his latest piece of jewelry held no weight for a policeman who continuously left his gun behind before reporting for his shifts. He thought he would be relegated to writing speeding tickets for the rest of his life.

And he would have if fate had not intervened.

The former low ranking Officer Riley hit a hot streak that even he couldn't explain. Three days in a row, he arrested a different criminal on the most wanted list, all former unsolved cases enduring over five years, responsible for driving the department absolutely insane. Victor didn't do anything special. He definitely didn't outthink his superiors. He just happened to be in the right place at the right time. His recent success made the other officers suspicious, rightly so because Victor's greatest asset up until then was his innate ability to expedite trips to Dunkin Donuts with an order for over 50 people. For so long he was an armed glorified intern.

Now he was Sergeant Victor Riley. The moving up ceremony lasted two and a half minutes. Only one witness was present to see him accept his newest medal, but the rite of passage was legitimate nonetheless. Captain Paul Cook shook his hand and told him to keep up the good work, which he had every intention of doing as long as there was that something to point him in the right direction.

Sergeant Riley found himself on the steps of a stranger's home for a reason he couldn't explain, brought there by forces outside of his control. It was up to him to solve the mystery. He had to figure out why he was about to arrest the person within without any evidence to suspect.

He knocked on the gray front door of the stranger's home. As he waited, Victor studied his surroundings. The rose bushes abutting against the garage were inviting. All of the bedroom windows weren't keeping any secrets, as if there was nothing for them to hide. Even the rustic railing summoned visitors to the door with promises of support up the stoop. Victor wondered what kind of criminal he was about to arrest. Based upon how nice the house appeared, Victor presumed that the homeowner wasn't a lowlife murderer. Maybe a rapist posing as a normal neighbor with an affinity for gardening and playing with the neighborhood kids. Maybe a high profile corporate MVP secretly embezzling millions. Sergeant Victor Riley wasn't intelligent enough to diagnose the case without meeting the specimen in question. He needed more help than what was already provided.

"Open up. The police."

The door immediately swung open to expose a nervous,

confused man shirtless and covered with tattoos, the most attractive being the wings of a bald eagle wrapped around the neck as if he were being choked. He was sweating profusely, obvious that he had just taken a time-out from some sort of cardio workout. Victor misconstrued his perspiration as a signal for admission of guilt.

"The police? Can I help you?"

"What's your name?"

"Walter. What's it to you?"

Victor had to make it seem like he knew what he was talking about, compelling the potential criminal to incriminate himself, and because he was in the right place at the right time, thanks to an unexplained outside factor, he could collect all of the accolades and maybe leap up to detective status faster than anybody else on the force. That was how he solved the prior cases that made him sergeant.

"Why don't you tell me why I'm here?" the officer with the hot streak said. Victor gripped his gun in the holster just in case.

"I don't have to answer no questions," Walter spat. "I ain't did nothin' wrong."

This was going to be harder than Victor initially thought. He wished there was a setting on his GPS that told him why his destinations were so important to follow. It would make his life so much easier, and hasten his second medal ceremony.

"We had complaints from your neighbors about a disturbance."

Walter and Victor looked around to confirm the accusation. There were no neighbors to account for. Not another house was in sight. Victor should have done his homework. He wasn't too bright.

"Um, I mean..."

"I don't know nothing, but don't you need a warrant or something to ask me these questions?"

He was definitely guilty of something. Inspector Riley couldn't decide what. If he acted like a real cop, then maybe he would have checked the inside of Walter's garage, run the license plate number of the non-distinctive pale green midsize Camry with a brown trim hibernating inside, and catch a dangerous kidnapper making headline news all over the nation.

A hero. He could see the front page of the Daily News: *Captain Riley Saves Man With Alzheimer's.*

"You're under arrest," Victor explained while reaching for the cuffs.

Victor didn't have any probable cause, but he didn't need any because he had his GPS telling him that he had reached his destination, which meant that Sergeant Victor Riley was standing at an unsolved crime scene. It hadn't let him down yet. There was no reason not to trust his navigator.

"You're making a big mistake!" Walter shouted. "I ain't done nothing wrong."

Walter wasn't cooperating. Victor didn't want to resort to physical force to apprehend him. Despite his ranking, Victor wasn't a very good cop.

CHAPTER EIGHTEEN

Some nights, Rebecca wished she were under the train, tied to the rails by a mustached stranger, counting every passing freight car overhead, hoping for inevitability. Most nights, Rebecca dreamed of being on the train, tempted and kidnapped by the sexy unknown, looking forward to starting over. On this particular night, and possibly for the first time, she was content with being stuck behind the train, living in the moment, prolonged by however long it took to see the caboose's caboose.

She almost felt like Atom did on the stalled Ferris wheel.

Almost.

Rebecca would have preferred to be dancing as her GPS suggested. For the first time, Walter's navigator offered a more favorable destination for her and Atom to peruse than what she had planned to do for their late morning.

She wasn't on vacation and definitely had no time for ballroom dancing. Her mission had always been to win back Atom's memories with or without the help from Walter's GPS. She appreciated what it had accomplished for her, which most recently included a cryptic note from a psychic medium possibly possessing the answers to Atom's freedom; however, it was time for her to take control of the wheel and finish the job herself. No more pit stops to Walter's preprogrammed destinations. Why the circus, a hypnotist, and a ghost whisperer would be addresses stored in his car's GPS, Rebecca didn't want to know. She never thought there was any more to Walter than the shallow lowlife on public display she learned to despise. What past demons was he looking to exorcise at his preprogrammed destinations?

I have no one to go dancing with anyway, Rebecca sulked, trying to justify her decision not to follow.

The navigator wanted Rebecca to head north, but that would be going out of her way. Or so she assumed. Rebecca avoided every proposed turn and resorted to foldout maps she bought from a passing gas station, which she hid from the navigator's sight, as if she were cheating on her comfortable routine. For the first time in her life, she was certain of her destination. This was where she should have been going all along.

She also made the decision that if she happened to be wrong, just in case, then it was back to the nursing home to face the consequences of her actions, even from her co-workers, who were more frightening to face than the authorities. This was her last opportunity for a meaningful relationship. Everything rested on Atom's ability to remember. If Alzheimer's stole Rebecca's only friend, then she and loneliness would turn each other in and be jailbait roomies until the end of time.

Atom's health was deteriorating exponentially. His ill will became very apparent to Rebecca on the latest leg of their road trip when he showed little interest in eating and had a hard time swallowing and breathing. She began to realize that maybe her excursion away from the nursing home was doing more harm to him than the naively expected good. Atom stopped verbally responding completely. The reruns of *Casablanca* shut down. Atom would be waiting forever for the next screening. Rebecca also noted a remarkable loss in motor and sensory abilities. The nurse inside her tried to get Atom to follow her finger with his eyes, but he was too slow to keep up. The hypnotist would have had a hard time putting him under again. She was running out of time.

It was a four-hour drive. Walter's GPS was going stir-crazy the entire way like an annoying child continuously crying out, "Are we there yet?" Little Miss Fugitive finally felt safe from the local news. She was proving to be very good at running away.

The editor's office at the *International Journal of Quantum Chemistry* was a pigpen. Hundreds of old volumes of the industry acclaimed magazine carpeted the floors and plastered the walls, plugging the cracks and holes allowing in the elements, literally. Models of the credits in the periodic table of elements hung from the ceiling like an experiment in bad taste. Atom's head knocked into the hydrogen and nitrogen dangling from the air conditioning duct, providing the necessary energy for what Atom used to define as electron leaps. Rebecca was amazed with how less professional and cluttered a placed that dealt in the sciences looked compared to the sterile hypnotist and psychic offices. It should have been the other way around.

Rebecca and Atom sat at the editor-in-chief desk, a beautiful stained mahogany piece, waiting for the IJQC's editor to grace them with his presence. Rebecca squeezed the note from beyond the grave, continuing to hope that it translated into a schoolyard double-dutch rhyme proclaiming eternal friendship.

"Seven-two-three-eight-six," Rebecca had memorized.

"When this trip is over, we'll go dancing," Rebecca told Atom while trying her best to hold back the tears from making a preemptive display. She was tired of crying, but there was no better release for her emotions.

Rebecca was so sad and lonely.

"Goddamn it, it is you," a heavyset man in the twilight of his career said while entering the room, ducking under the oxygen and calcium formations, as if disproving of Atom's energy leap theory. "When the receptionist told me who was here, I didn't believe her. I had to see for myself."

The man, who Rebecca surmised was the IJQC's editor-in-chief, might as well have had his foot in his mouth because he was running a marathon with his dialogue at a million words per minute. His breath smelled as if that were the case, too.

Rebecca stood up and introduced herself, but Mr. Editor only seemed to be interested in Atom's presence, completely awe-stricken by his blank stare.

"I'm his nurse. He has Alzheimer's and cannot comprehend anything."

"So then, nothing has changed."

"What is that supposed to mean?" Rebecca asked suspiciously, protecting her investment in friendship like a rare stone. "Who are you?"

Rebecca wished Atom could stand up for himself. She had enough trouble as it was explaining her own story.

"Ross Smith," the editor said, continuing to inspect Rebecca's rare stone to assess its value. All he found were timeworn defects, which were compromising its measure like a worthless rock. Ross was fascinated by the flashbacks. He had no interest in Rebecca. Like everyone else she met, Rebecca was ignored.

"Do you know him?" Rebecca asked.

"Do I know him? He made my career."

Rebecca's eyes lit up. She knew Atom discovered something important to the chemistry world when he was teaching at the University, but she didn't know to what extent.

"What did he discover?"

"Allegedly?"

Rebecca's comfortable thoughts were thrown for a surprise.

"Atomic memory," Ross explained. "He figured out a way to store bits of information using silicon atoms. He developed the first prototype interface of memory with a storage density one million times greater than a CD-ROM. Genius, really. Who would have thought to evaporate gold onto a silicon wafer for the ultimate means of housing data? Just think of being able to store all of the written words in history on a cube measuring just one two-hundredths of an inch. That was Professor Feynman's vision forty years ago, and now it's a reality.

There is no limit to data storage. We will never be without information again."

Rebecca was proud of her patient. She didn't really understand the accomplishment, but it sounded impressive.

"How come I've never heard of this?"

"There are still some hitches from realizing the full extent of the technology. Atom could never find the appropriate vacuum to create the memory. It haunted him."

The nurse was still confused and still impressed. She was glad her GPS recommended the IJQC as the next destination. It was a valuable learning experience. It was an unforgettable bonding experience with her best friend.

"Atomic memory, huh?"

"Now, do you want to hear the real story?" Ross asked.

"What do you mean? What did you just tell me?"

Ross sidled up to her. She could smell the foot odor from his breath. Their proximity was overwhelming.

"Why are you here?" Ross wondered. He was serious. There was no playful tone to convey a forthcoming light-hearted conversation.

"I want to help him remember before it's too late."

Ross stood up, releasing the hypnotic hold he had on Rebecca with his tone, and walked around his mahogany desk so he could access his computer.

"Honey, I don't think you'd be helping. Don't you know things happen for a reason?" Ross continued, as his fingers danced on the keyboard. "There are some things you have no right meddling your business in. And, if I may speak for Atom here, I think this is one situation that is beyond your control. So, I'll ask you again. Why are you here?"

She thought for a while. Did Rebecca really think she was helping? Why else would she travel the four hours to be at the IJQC headquarters? Would it make a difference to Atom's sorry excuse for a life if she uncovered the past secrets to his success? Maybe she wasn't there for him after all.

"I want to help him remember before it's too late," Rebecca stoically repeated, her brain still trying to process the reality of her answer.

Ross rolled his eyes and spun the computer monitor around so that it faced Rebecca's crippling dishonesty. The desktop displayed an issue of the IJQC that was over 30 years old. Rebecca was rendered numb with disbelief, but the image was unmistakably clear. On the front page of the journal was a picture of Atom, the associated headline reading: *Fraudulent Son Steals Father's Findings.*

"You wanted to know," Ross remarked.

Rebecca couldn't understand. She tried to read the blackmailing article, but her languishing sanity wouldn't allow her to comprehend its meaning. She compared the picture of the young, healthy, and cheating Atom on screen with the dying old man feigning innocence sitting next to her. He seemed to be completely unaware of the article's accusations of him, but Rebecca didn't know what to believe anymore.

"I don't understand," Rebecca managed to muster.

"I wrote that thirty-eight years ago," Ross gleamed. "It saved the publication and bought me this beautiful mahogany desk. What do you think?"

"Is it true?"

"Well, the desk came three months later, but..."

"The article," she interrupted. "Is it true?"

Here came Ross and his feet breath again to sit on top of Rebecca to have one of his famous sober conversations. Rebecca was fighting all types of emotions.

"Atom's father was a great scientist, but a horrible father," Ross explained to Rebecca, who wasn't prepared for the long-winded answer she was about to receive. "Consider the name he gave his son. If that isn't abuse, I don't know what is. He treated Atom like one of his scientific experiments. However, instead of blasting this Atom with electrical impulses, he used a much more powerful tactic, forcing him to follow his own professional footsteps using what some might deem psychological torture, abating his only son's shelf life until he was rendered helpless and hopeless."

Rebecca imagined Atom locked in the dark musty basement hunched over a Bunsen burner longing to play kickball with the other children in his neighborhood while his father ordered him to mix various unstable compounds without safety goggles.

"Is that why his father would be apologizing?" Rebecca asked, remembering the incident at the hypnotist's office and the yellow flowers Atom was presented with from a restless, guilt-ridden ghost, courtesy of the psychic medium.

"He wanted to be an actor. He did the best impressions of Humphrey Bogart." Ross smiled as he reminisced. "That was the only time I saw him excited."

Rebecca's eyes lit up.

Atom can remember.

"But as his time progressed, leading him farther away from self-autonomy, he became more and more like his father. He was hard on his students. And I don't mean unpredictable pop quizzes hard. He broke them down, made them fear his class, which was more like a concentration camp. How do I know? I was one of his students. Half of the semester he came to class piss drunk."

Rebecca wondered how Ross' explanation could be boiled down to the 72386 code inscribed on her note. She was learning more about Atom than she ever knew in the years nursing him out of Alzheimer's.

"I've heard enough. So what?" Rebecca interrupted.

"It was the scientific breakthrough of the millennium and the accolades Atom received, not to mention the financial rewards, were not warranted."

"Why didn't his father come out and set the story straight?"

"He was murdered before Atom was published."

"What are you saying? Atom killed his father over some irrelevant scientific equations?"

"There's more to the story, goddamn it!" Atom screamed, springing up into an upright position, eyes wide and completely attentive, no longer fighting his mind and body to function properly in the automatic gear. "Check my pants."

Rebecca, the nurse, rushed to Atom's side, praying she inadvertently found the cure to Alzheimer's at the IJQC's headquarters amongst the ceiling decorations of the periodic table. There was no better place for the cure to hide.

"Keep talking," she urged her patient.

"They found an unregistered gun in the glove compartment of his car after his father's murder," Ross interrupted. "He was asleep behind the wheel on the side of the highway when it was discovered. I'm no investigator; I just report the facts."

"There were other mitigating circumstances," Atom barked at Ross.

Rebecca cried. She was unsure if this was the right time for Atom to beat his crippling disease. The memories trying to fight their way back seemed to be more aggressive than the Alzheimer's.

"Do you know what you're saying?" Rebecca asked, refusing to believe that her only friend was a murderer. She wouldn't be able to recover if it turned out that the person she dedicated all her time trying to get to know was a cold-blooded killer. "Atom shot his father to death for his life's work?"

"Not according to the legal system. He had one hell of a lawyer, not to mention a fuck-up cop making the arrest. Check his wrists. I'm sure you've seen them. Atom, the great scientist, tried to take the coward's way out, but couldn't even do that right. I uncovered all of his father's original handwritten documents about the scientific breakthrough Atom claimed to have discovered and reprinted them in the IJQC. And it exposed him."

"That still doesn't explain why he would kill his father. Atom please set the record straight. Defend yourself," Rebecca pleaded. "Tell this man it isn't true. Tell *me* it isn't true."

"Gray matter doesn't even matter. We all eat pudding under purple moons."

Rebecca suddenly clutched her stomach in pain

and fell over. "How do you live with yourself?" Rebecca asked, trying to breathe in-between the sharp quakes of pain ripping through her abdomen. She was mad at everybody, including Atom, who appeared so innocent behind his disease.

"Why are you here?" Ross asked again.

She couldn't blame Walter or the GPS on this one.

Rebecca didn't know what to tell him. She really believed she could help cure a deadly disease, but it wasn't Alzheimer's she was really trying to cure. She was looking to heal an equally noxious affliction. Loneliness.

"I don't know why I'm here," Rebecca confessed. "But let me ask you a question. Did you accomplish everything you set out to accomplish from printing that article? Are you happy with how everything turned out?"

Ross looked over at Atom who was suffering but didn't know it. He would have been suffering even more if he had the ability to remember all of the infectious memories that Ross and Rebecca were digging up, which turned him into his vituperative father he grew up despising.

"Atom knew exactly what he was doing back then, and maybe he has escaped the punishment he deserves…"

"I don't want to hear anymore!" Rebecca screamed, covering her ears with her hands, a juvenile attempt at listening to the fossils of her past.

"If you think you're helping by forcing him to remember his past, you better be prepared for what might happen."

Rebecca shoved the psychic's note deeper into her pocket.

It was time to go home. The mission was aborted

without accomplishing the end goal. She was going to return the car back to Walter and Atom back to the nursing home, both in worse condition than how she borrowed them.

Even she was no better off.

The tears flowed again. It was back to masking her true emotions like an enslaved robot while engaging in pointless teatimes with Atom, who she would never trust again as being the true friend she built him up to be.

Could all that Ross said about Atom be true? Rebecca feared. *Would it matter either way? Why would it affect their relationship?*

"We all make mistakes in the past that we have to live with forever," Rebecca reminded herself. "Except Atom. He is exempt from that responsibility."

Rebecca was stuck trying to look ahead through the rearview mirror.

"One more stop."

Rebecca puked all over Ross' beautiful mahogany desk. Atom remembered nothing after all.

CHAPTER NINETEEN

Jason found himself at another dubious location, thanks to you know whom. He never parted with his GPS as he promised himself he would. As wicked and undependable as Jason's free online gift was, it was also equally persuasive and seductive. It reminded him of someone he used to know. To make the situation even worse, the navigator took him past three different garbage dumps as if daring his feeble owner to follow through with his own decisions.

A tease.

During the entire ride to another unknown destination, Jason envisioned starting a family with the mysterious Strykowski at the bar. His potential cousin. They could live happily ever after, comfortable in knowing that their spouse is a perfect match for organ donations and blood transfusions.

A proud way to keep the family name alive, he scoffed. "What were you thinking?" Jason asked his machine.

If the GPS could have answered without barking directional commands, then it might have asked Jason what was wrong with the two blondes flanking Sheryl at the bar.

Jason used to know how to have fun. Up through the time he graduated college, Jason was a three-sport athlete. He played in recreational baseball leagues on weekends, frequented the golf course during the late weekday afternoon twilight specials, and ran five miles every morning at the lake before starting his day. Like most other twenty-somethings, Jason had a curiosity for life, wanting to experience all that it had to offer so that the path leading him into the future wasn't so naive. Jason was also an avid reader, played the drums in a garage band with his roommates, and traveled the world.

As the saying goes, it's all fun and games until someone gets a job. He didn't have time to be curious anymore after law school. He traded that privilege in for a meaningless title and money he had no use for. Jason slowly allowed himself to be swallowed whole by society's limitations on freedom. He didn't put up a fight either. Nobody ever did. He simply accepted his fate as man's unnatural evolution. He was now a former athlete too old for baseball, too busy for golf, and too tired for running. He always sensed he was getting worse at everything he used to be skilled at doing, but it wasn't until most recently it started to bother him. Life wasn't like riding a bike. At least not for Jason and the millions of other corporate slogs who hadn't peddled against the wind in decades. If fun wasn't sitting through 10 hours of court depositions in search of the one loophole to acquit the guilty, then fun was definitely not on Jason's destination list, which was why he actively avoided the best reasons people entered into relationships.

His navigation system was trying really hard to reverse the curse, but the infected agent seemed to be suffering from dementia. He thought the navigator's selfless cure was the debilitating curse. When you've been employed for so long, it's difficult to tell which is the life worth tracking down.

There was so much more on the line than Jason's offspring. His night may have meant more if he had just gone dancing.

Their latest excursion offered a different kind of fun, but for the first time, the GPS was thinking on the same wavelength as Jason. It offered him an easy way of prolonging the Strykowski tradition without having to partake in any of the backbreaking work that made him appear phony and desperate.

He was in the waiting room of the GPS' desired destination with alluring magazines to prepare him for his shortcut to fatherhood.

In the end, everything boiled down to the hand. All Jason had to do was rub it against something hard as if he were a Boy Scout starting his first fire, and the recipe to his future would spill out.

Jason was at a sperm bank waiting to make a deposit.

It was just like being a ghostwriter. He would be the author of the child while someone else much more qualified took all the credit, exactly how he always envisioned it would be. If Jason wanted a relationship without the dreaded "L" word, then this was his express ticket to that desolate destination.

The perfect plan and Jason was taking all the credit away from his GPS. Somewhere, somehow, there would be another Strykowski offspring populating the population, brought up by parents who actually cared...and loved. This plan provided the best interest of all active parties involved.

There was always that one variable to his plan that he had no control over. He remembered hearing this one doctor explain on TV that gene manipulation was the wave of the future for all of the control freak parents unsatisfied with Mother Nature's design. The doctor forecasted that one day soon people would be able to preorder their custom baby as if they were shopping for clothes in a magazine.

Gene manipulation was normally performed to prevent the proliferation of certain diseases. The technology was available to adjust the X- and Y-chromosomes of the fetus' DNA so its gender could be predetermined like the paint color of a car. Jason would never have to worry about fathering females ill equipped with the ability to sustain a family name. He had to find out if this was a service that the sperm bank offered. Was gene manipulation an add-on cost like ordering an Extra Value meal at McDonalds?

"Excuse me," Jason said to the receptionist upon entering the sperm bank. "If I were to say, do the whole you know what into a cup, do we have any control over how my goods are packaged and delivered?"

"I don't understand what you mean, sir."

The sperm bank receptionist had to deflect a lot of interesting questions on the job. The upcoming inquiry from Jason might have been her most unusual.

"Do you offer assurance to the provider that the product will furnish into his expectations?" Jason asked, as if he were dealing with a business client, trying to nail down a multi-million dollar deal.

"You're going to have to be more specific. I don't understand your question."

Jason sighed. He was going to have to be straight with her, just like how he was with the women at the speed-dating forum.

"Gene manipulation," he said. "I'm kinda looking for someone to raise my son. I have no use for a girl. It would really help me out of a jam."

The receptionist didn't know how to respond. She was right to think he was nuts, but instead of feeding his curiosity with more questions, she continued to deflect.

"Take a seat, sir. The doctor can answer all of your questions."

Jason's GPS wanted him to start having fun, which he wasn't going to accomplish by arguing with the receptionist about the ethics of genetic control.

The paperwork he was issued laid out the guidelines. Jason would be compensated $100 for a plastic cup filled with erotic imagination. He would also have to submit a picture and bio for the official sperm bank yearbook, which was regularly read by anatomically handicapped wanna-be parents. For lack of motivation, Jason used the same picture and bio from his online dating profile.

No matter how hard he tried, Jason wouldn't even

allow himself to enjoy the x-rated magazines at the sperm bank. All he could think about was Veronica Maine.

She would forever be remembered as the girl on Jason's desktop.

They met in high school. Jason was too young to have already adopted his cynical attitude on love. They instantly became a couple. Veronica may not have been the prettiest girl by horny teenage boy standards. Her smooth, clear cheeks and her long, dark hair complemented a perfectly shaped body, which was probably too mature for her age. Jason was infatuated, but it didn't begin and end with her looks. They also shared the same interests; running together in the park after class, tutoring one another on different subjects, even sharing music mixes.

Jason believed he was going to marry her.

It was prom night, and the seemingly happy couple looked like they belonged on top of a wedding cake. As the night began to fade, Jason anxiously anticipated the last dance, a slow number designed to lead to their first kiss, which he practiced repeatedly in his mind. Instead, as Veronica and Jason held each other in a slow, awkward back and forth rock, Veronica performed open-heart surgery without any anesthesia.

"Jason, you know how I feel about you, and you know I will always be your friend…but we can't date. You're like a brother to me."

Jason didn't have to hear the rest. She explained how their friendship was too important to be risking in a serious relationship. All Jason could do was nod in agreement while trying not to crumble from disappointment as his mind ran away. He loved her. He thought she loved him. He had to concentrate really hard to finish their dance in silence. He must have stepped on her toes 100 times, as the last few measures of the dance song expired. Not all were unintentional.

The night continued in silence, and they never talked since. Their friendship that Veronica was so concerned with preserving vanished as if it were the last of an endangered species.

For so long he tried to remember that moment like the rehearsals he held in his mind prior to the big show. Recalling an imaginative first kiss on the dance floor was much healthier than reliving a nightmare. Reality eventually intervened to question the validity of his accounts of the past.

Jason vowed never to seek out the very emotion that was taken from him all those years ago.

He was still in love.

Jason stopped secretly stalking Veronica at her home 15 years ago. The picture on Jason's desktop would suffice.

"Mr. Strykowski, the doctor will see you now."

The receptionist ushered him down a long hallway, passing different examination rooms along the way. Jason didn't want to know what kind of self-implementing medical procedures were going on behind those doors. The magazines in the waiting room were involved. Jason knew firsthand, having already been issued his cup. It took him almost a half an hour to finish the procedure.

"Why wouldn't you want to have a baby girl?" the receptionist had to ask as they continued to shuffle down the hall together. "Are you one of those sexist pigs?"

Jason didn't feel like expounding upon his situation. He had no more energy to go into his 'save the endangered family' pitch. Besides, he could never discuss his mission when thoughts of Veronica swirled around in his head.

"I like girls," Jason rebutted, which probably didn't help his case against the sperm bank receptionist's sexist accusations.

"Last door to your left," she directed like his GPS.

Jason was right. He wasn't taken to another typical cum-stained examination room to sit on butcher paper. Room 127 was the doctor's personal office. Instead of having to wait another 20 minutes to see the doctor, like he would if he was in a regular examination room, the doctor was already in his office waiting for him. The roles were reversed. The only difference was he didn't have his pants around his ankles.

"I'm Dr. Mayo, the clinic's urologist," he greeted Jason from behind his desk. "Have a seat. Can I offer you anything?"

The receptionist left, closing the door behind her.

It was a beautiful office. Jason always believed that an office's status was determined by how nice the chair was behind the desk. Dr. Mayo reclined in a leather-upholstered centerpiece built for design and comfort.

If this were a movie or a book, then Jason would have entered the scene where the doctor tells him he only has three months left to live. Unfortunately, for Jason, this was real life. Even though he wasn't in mortal danger, the news the doctor was about to break to him made him wish his existence were set to a rapidly descending timer. He would have been better off dead.

"We reviewed your sample."

Jason sensed that something was amiss, assuming the

secretary enlightened the doctor about his sexist genetic experiments.

"I was only asking about genetically pre-selecting a gender because I saw a show about it on television not too long ago," Jason defended.

"Sorry, I don't follow, but you might want to know that you have oligospermia and therefore, we cannot accept your sperm donation."

"What is oligospermia? A low sperm count?"

"It's a little bit more complicated than that. A normal sperm count is twenty million or more sperm per millimeter of semen, and sixty percent of those sperm should have proper shape and mobility."

"What is my percentage of healthy sperm?" Jason asked, knowing that it couldn't be good. "Don't tell me I'm depleted."

Dr. Mayo pulled out a manila envelope and unearthed a small stack of papers for his personal review. "Our charts tell us that you're infertile."

Jason was stunned. The game was over. No more fun promised by his navigation system. The family's hopes of keeping the Strykowski name alive were officially dead. He was unequipped to meet the challenge.

"How?" Jason was barely able to muster.

"You have one extra X-chromosome," the doctor explained. "All fertile males must have one Y-chromosome, which you do not have."

Jason didn't know what to say. The doctor didn't realize that his flippant prognosis was spelling out the extinction of an entire family history.

"I can change my diet."

"I'm sorry. Your factors are not environmental and

cannot be reversed. This is a biological condition that you were born with."

The infertile Strykowski was too upset to appreciate the irony. Jason was the last living male Strykowski, pressured by the rest of his history-conscious family into procreating a baby male to keep the name and tradition alive. Ironically, the very same family that required he save them from the endangered species list, passed on a genetic disorder that prevented him from realizing their sustenance.

"How come nobody else in my family had this problem?"

"The code for this disease is written in all of your family's DNA, but it takes a rare protein to unlock it. You have that protein strand."

Jason should have felt relieved by the news. All these years, Jason thought that he was the problem. He never had any control over the situation to begin with.

"So you can understand why we have no use for your sample," Dr. Mayo said while closing Jason's chart. "This will not affect your sexual drive."

The doctor thought his last comment might lift Jason's spirits, but he would have to be sexually active in order to take full advantage of the one perk.

The destination seemed so promising until he learned he had an extra X-chromosome marring his ability to have a child he could pass onto another couple like a hot potato. He didn't know how to feel toward his navigator and probably wouldn't until he knew where their next destination was going to be.

Jason remembered the promise he made to his father

on his deathbed and winced knowing he would never be able to fulfill it.

He left Dr. Mayo's office feeling less of a man, dreading having to pass the receptionist and her judgmental glare. There would be no genetic experiments for Jason. Not in this lifetime. He wanted to be taken away by his GPS so he wouldn't have to break the news to his mother. She would still find a way to blame him for his infertility.

Jason could hear her now.

There had to be somewhere he could go instead of back home.

CHAPTER TWENTY

"You have reached your destination."

He heard that one before.

Norman pulled onto the shoulder of a desolate highway, exactly where Pamela wanted him to be. After almost being run down by a freight train, Norman allowed his GPS to take him as far away from his near death experience as possible. Luckily, his car keys took him to his next destination and not the loaded magnum. Either way, his GPS wanted him dead. At first, Pamela brought him to the gates of a cemetery, which Norman thought was a morbid way of telling him he should have been killed on the rumbling tracks, but when he drove up to the tombstone that Pamela wanted him to see, he realized there was more to the destination than met the eye.

Here lies Nina Bates, the tombstone read.

"That's my mother."

The dates on the headstone said, *1928 to 1950.*

She was 22 when she died, complications during childbirth. Norman never met his mother, and his father never spoke about her. She made the ultimate sacrifice for his existence.

Norman assumed his father's lack of memory was alcohol related. It wasn't until little Norman escaped to a life in the circus did he begin to understand the gaping hole in his past. He thought it was scabbing over until he found himself in front of a 60-year-old headstone breaking through earth's epidermis.

This was the first time Norman ever visited his mother's grave. He didn't know what he was supposed to get out of the experience and he never blamed his mother for leaving. If she were alive when he grew up, maybe he would have been a normal kid who played Little League and came home every evening with skinned knees. He could have been a reputable contribution to society like a chemist or a botanist. She could have offset many of the problems he had with his father. They could have been a normal family.

He was the only soul breathing at the cemetery, but it didn't distinguish him from the neighbors underneath him. A gentle breeze consoled a weeping willow nearby.

"I suppose you're not in the market for a vacuum?" Norman asked his mother, trying in vain to start a conversation.

"Where were you?" Norman said. "No, I won't do it."

Norman argued with himself, a losing battle. He

paced in front of the headstone, trying to gather his thoughts.

"You died for me. And look where I am now. Look at the life I led. Do you still think you made the right decision? If you had to do it all over again, would you have me?"

He couldn't blame his mother. It wasn't her fault.

Why am I here?

"Was I supposed to be here? Anywhere? Am I one big mistake gone terribly wrong? I have nowhere to go. I'm so lost."

There was a fresh bouquet of flowers resting next to the granite headstone. Norman wondered who would have brought them to her; probably someone he should have known.

Even though he had reached his destination, Norman had a change of plans. Pamela wasn't going to be happy, but it was time to leave. Hoping to keep a memory, he grabbed the bouquet of flowers from the grave.

Now Norman found himself on the side of the road, nothing around for miles, but it was his destination. Pamela said so.

To his right was a seemingly endless grass field. There were no cars parading around license plates identifying his current state. There were no mile markers denoting his position on the road. All Norman knew was he couldn't be any farther away from the cemetery, Gloria's palm reading shop, or his childhood home. As long as Pamela was in control, Norman was never lost.

Norman was in the middle of nowhere, where he normally felt most at home. He was certain that Pamela wanted him exactly where he was because every time he attempted to continue traversing the road, she would recalculate the directions to their destination and bring them right back to the same spot on the side of the highway. Like a fool in love, Norman turned around on Pamela's requests every time without an argument.

He was still bothered by the fact that she wanted him to reconnect with a mother he never met as if it would help him find his way into the future or accept his repressive childhood with his abusive father. What Norman should have been more worried about was why she kept offering him the coward's way out of a life not lived. The gun and the train tracks should have made him a little bit more suspicious or careful with the next turn he made in his life.

All he could think about was his father. He hadn't seen him in over 30 years, yet he would forever feel haunted by him as long as he survived in Norman's memory. The lonely traveling salesman envisioned the murder, his Power Hum Vac 3500X acting as the perfect accomplice, his job the perfect excuse for the impromptu visit back home. However, since Papa Tate only existed in the sanctity of Norman's mind, the procedure would result in a murder/suicide. It would be a small price to pay for freedom.

He remembered the gun. Norman imagined the cold mouth of the weapon French kissing his forehead as it prepared for the ultimate assassination attempt. Norman wouldn't be the only innocent victim.

"Who is the gun for?"

Norman was tired of having the gun on his mind. And especially his father.

"I'm sorry. I still don't know why, no matter how long

I search for the answers, but I'm sorry," Norman cried. "I'm so sorry, Dad."

Norman pounded his temples, his cheeks glowing.

"I'm lost and I want to go home. Please let me come home."

It was futile. The only way for Norman to witness a more lyrical version of his past was to have it translated through the REM cycle.

Even though it had been over 12 hours since he last ate and two nights since he slept in a warm bed, Norman decided to wait it out on the side of the road. He unlocked his seatbelt, reclined his seat, and closed his eyes.

Sleep and dreams. They don't go hand in hand. Although, Norman required an unconscious mental state in order to experience the hopes of an alternate reality. While sleeping on the side of the road with Pamela, Norman dreamed of his final destination; a world that not even his bagless vacuum could fabricate.

The title of his dream would have been, "A World Without People" starring only Norman with no supporting characters to interact. The setting was an empty space, devoid of piss catchers with wet pants and dirt bags with clean carpets. It was just Norman and Pamela driving sans destination until the magnum hiding out in the glove compartment had something to say about the situation.

The one thing about Norman's dreams was that they were only dreams. He couldn't translate them into a language relevant to the real world no matter how deeply he concentrated or how much he slept. There were always the inconveniences of his species to foil his plans for a barren world when he was awake and vulnerable.

A utopia for the insane.

Three hours passed. A respectable nap of much needed hours deposited in Norman's depleted energy bank. Nevertheless, he was still on the side of the road, still alone with his navigation system not telling him to make any moves. He should have been delighted. It was the closest he would ever get to living out his dreams. There was no sign of life for miles.

A world without people.

Norman was getting cold as the sun set across the grass field. It was almost 9:00. He was still without rations.

He looked around and smiled.

"I did it."

A World Without People, starring Norman Tate, became a reality. Pamela finally brought him to a place that agreed with him. No one-armed Ralphs or abusive fathers to worry about, and Gloria wasn't around to judge the lines in his hands.

He had reached his destination. Norman had no intentions of leaving the side of the highway. Everything that he ever wanted was already within his grasp. All outside influences vanished from existence.

Pamela and Norman didn't need to be in conversation to justify their relationship. The silence was anything but awkward. They were past the phoniness. The pointless "how was your day" and "what did you do at work" conversations were well beneath them. It was a much more sophisticated relationship, one in which Pamela barked her orders and Norman faithfully submitted.

Peace and quiet, Norman relished. He was alone.

The dream didn't last very long. It was swallowed whole by a pair of approaching headlights burning through the darkness. He should have known his utopia was too good to be true. No matter where he went, Norman couldn't break away from the world and its annoying citizens.

Norman and Pamela would have to postpone their date. There was an intruder present to turn their dream into a nightmare. The headlights grew in the reflection of the rearview mirror as they traveled down the road, one faint light becoming two very distinct beams of an approaching automobile. It would have helped if lampposts illuminated the highway, but there wasn't enough traffic to justify the expense. The headlights were attached to nothing but darkness until they were close enough to decipher their real host supplying the power.

The approaching vehicle was a police car, the rats of the population. They would be the first members of his society that Norman would erase into oblivion in the construction of his peopleless world.

Norman's worst nightmare.

The uniformed driver activated all of the squad car's colorful lights decorating the top of the roof as he approached. Norman was being pulled over without being pulled over.

"No, no, please leave me alone."

He couldn't have any time to himself. There always somebody around to remind him that a world without people was nothing more than an unreachable dream.

The police officer wasn't alone. Norman noticed a figure sitting in the caged backseat of the squad car. It was hard to make out any specific physical features because the officer's headlights were shining too brightly into Norman's car, but he could definitely make out another person. Even though all he had to do was face forward and wait for the fuzz to reprimand the lonely traveler, Norman couldn't help but look backward into the light. Every time he did, he was blinded. He didn't learn.

The policeman stepped out of his car and slowly walked along the side of the highway, his hand by the holster, not knowing what to expect. He brought with him a pair of deep pounding footsteps to feign confidence and authority while carrying a handheld version of the car's headlights.

Norman rolled down the window as the police officer approached, also not knowing what to expect. They stared at each other in silence.

"Can I help you, Officer?"

"You're under arrest," he said while reaching for the handcuffs. "Anything you say or do can be held against you in the court of law."

"What did I do wrong? I didn't know it was a felony to pull over on the side of the road if you're tired."

Norman noticed a badge of honor attached to the officer's uniform, displaying his rank and name: Sergeant Riley. Norman could now attach a name to the idiot incriminating him for a crime he didn't commit.

Sergeant Riley always received the same reaction to his presence whenever he was about to go in for the kill and he never knew how to respond. At least this time he remembered to recite the Miranda rights.

"What did I do wrong?" Norman repeated.

Sergeant Victor Riley didn't know the answer. His GPS did. Why else would it have commanded him to stop behind Norman's car on the shoulder of an abandoned highway? It still hadn't steered him wrong yet.

"Why don't you tell me?" Riley responded, shining the flashlight in Norman's eyes until they burned out tears, which the bumbling officer falsely interpreted as a guilty reaction to his question.

Norman was guilty of many things in the past and probably should have been locked out of society for his own good, a mandatory timeout for a little while. There wasn't anything illegal about parking on the side of the road. Sergeant Riley was going to have his hands full trying to decipher this one.

"This your vehicle?" Riley asked, believing he was onto something.

"If I give you my license and registration, will you leave me the fuck alone?" Norman barked back, tired of people. Dumb, annoying people like Victor.

The newly appointed sergeant reached his hand into the car through the open window and opened the driver's side door, against Norman's will. While Norman and the police officer wrestled for control of the car door, Pamela reminded him of his destination like a broken record.

If only Norman could remember the gun hiding in the glove compartment, but his magnum wasn't nearly as talkative as his GPS. It didn't matter. Victor won their tug of war game on the car door and swung it wide open. He grabbed the back of Norman's shirt and pulled him onto the road.

"If you're not going to cooperate, we'll have to do this my way!" the sergeant yelled, pulling out the handcuffs.

He shoved Norman's head into the gravel until his cheeks pushed into his nostrils. Victor was too dumb to be worried about police brutality, evidenced by the blood trickling out of Norman's nose staining the highway.

Besides, he trusted every word of his navigation system. Just like Norman.

Victor twisted Norman's arms behind his back, which would have made even Ralph, the one-armed master contortionist, wince in pain. With the handcuffs securely locked around his wrists, Sergeant Riley kicked Norman in the gut before yanking him back to a standing position by his hair.

"Let's go," Victor declared, ushering him into the police car, not concerned with assisting his head safely into the backseat.

The police officer always seeming to be in the right place at the right time made his second arrest of the day, both sitting side-by-side in the backseat of the squad car. He still didn't know why either of them was under arrest, but like all the others he brought into the precinct, they were bound to check out. One for aiding and abetting, and the other for destruction of private property.

He would probably be promoted. Again.

"Where we off to now, motherfucker?" Walter snapped at Sergeant Riley.

"I don't know yet. It's not up to me."

They sat there in silence, Norman trying to regain his breath and his faith in humanity, Walter trying to escape the handcuffs attaching him to the car door, and Victor trying to justify how he went about his profession.

"After one-quarter mile, turn left," Victor's GPS said, which made Norman long for Pamela and her conciliatory voice.

"Detective Riley here I come," the sergeant said.

He pulled back onto the road and drove off, passing Norman's car, which was now completely under Pamela's domain. Exactly what she wanted. As they passed, the Power Hum Vac 3500X with the odor shield and the self-propelled rotating brush roll cried for his companion, wishing it could take back all that it said.

"Where are we going?" Walter asked again.

Victor didn't respond. He didn't know how. Their next location wasn't up to him. Norman's car was becoming a distant memory in the rearview mirror.

Pamela, the vacuum, and the magnum achieved something that Norman could never attain; no matter how hard he tried, which began with two scars on his wrists. A world without people. At least for a little while.

They could argue over how people are becoming more like their machines. Or vice versa.

CHAPTER TWENTY-ONE

The water was cold. As usual. Rebecca's dangling feet were shriveling as fast as Atom's chances of surviving the end of their trip together.

His skin was yellow with disease and Rebecca's GPS thought her childhood lake house would be the perfect ointment for his ailment. Atom shook uncontrollably and moaned in pain to debate the favorability of the destination. His smile vanished as soon as they crossed the state line, reversing its shape the closer they drove into another memory.

Rebecca was back at the lake house. It wasn't her idea. She would rather return Walter's car and bring herself in to face the consequences of her actions, no longer with a desire to pursue the meaning of the psychic medium's note translated from Atom's dead, abusive father. Rebecca felt tired and defeated. The lonely nurse couldn't understand why she was directed closer to her own memories the harder she searched for Atom's.

Rebecca was ashamed of Atom's past behavior. An alcoholic and a cheat. A liar. A killer. She hoped life was predetermined, controlled by a giant navigation system from the heavens so that Atom didn't have to accept responsibility for his actions. Rebecca should have known all about taking the blame for circumstances out of her own jurisdiction. That was what the psychic medium tried to explain to the fake Rebecca at the supernatural reading.

The water was glistening under the moon, and the stars looked down on the lonely nurse and her dying patient sitting at the edge of a wooden dock, their feet saturated. Wrinkled.

Somewhere in the starlight's twinkle was the beginning of time.

The lake house, which was dressed more like a hut or a shack, postured behind them, a safe distance from a ground attack from the water rats living in the lake, but it was a shell of its former self, hiding out in embarrassment from the elements with a judgmental memory. A consequence of time without human intervention. The rotting wood foundation fell victim to the schizophrenic seasons and the neighboring termites. The windows were painted with a coating of nature's forgotten wonders. The uneven wooden steps and the similarly manufactured platform of the back patio where Rebecca's family used to cook their summer dinners now appeared dangerously unsturdy. An old and broken bicycle leaned against the house for support. The lawn. There were so many memories for Rebecca on the lawn of the lake house, from playing wiffleball with her brother to rolling around with Patton, the family dog. Now, the lawn was overgrown and unkempt, the memories lost among the high, suffocating grasses and weeds of time. Nature's Alzheimer's.

Rebecca didn't attempt a reunion tour of the lake house. She wouldn't find anything in there except for nauseating dead-end memory triggers. There were plenty of ghosts at the end of the dock to occupy her thoughts. The lake house, despite all of its pitfalls, managed to survive without people.

Atom, the human lake house with the overgrown lawn and the profane windows asphyxiating his memories, might as well have been on top of a stalled Ferris wheel enjoying his destination without the weight of past and the promise of future destinations pulling him apart.

It wasn't about Atom. It never was. His story was over a long time ago. It was up to Rebecca to learn a thing or two from his condition. She needed to find a Ferris wheel so she wouldn't have to hang in the balance.

To be in the moment. To not allow Walter's GPS to take her back. Rebecca had been stuck in reverse ever since she began teatime with Atom at the nursing home.

She needed to forget, but the more she fought Atom's Alzheimer's, the more she was forcefully reconnected with visions of her own history, plagiarized by others. Rebecca was ashamed of her past behavior. She was no different from Atom. They were the same person. An alcoholic and a cheat. A liar. A killer.

"The answer lies in the closet," Atom said.

There was one more story Rebecca needed to digest. She didn't care if Atom paid attention to her reminiscing. This tale was not a prescription against Alzheimer's. She remembered as if recalling a fugitive memory slowly finding its way back home. And Rebecca didn't have any control over the private screening.

* * * * *

It had been three weeks since insemination. Two-and-a-half since that embarrassing trip to the convenience store for a test she was sure she'd fail. The cashier was right to be concerned about ringing up such a grownup piece of merchandise for a 12-year-old girl.

"Is this for you?"

Little Rebecca prepared herself for such an inquisition. The barcode on the toothpaste-sized box enclosing the outlook to her future longed to be read like the lines on a palm, hoping she didn't screw up her rehearsed response.

"It's for my friend, Alex," Rebecca said, holding up a plastic doll missing an arm and the means to defend itself. "I think she might have twins."

The cashier shouldn't have been convinced, but rung up the piss catcher anyway. It wasn't in her job description to prejudge her customers based upon the purchases she stuffed into plastic bags for them. It was only a hobby.

Rebecca was only 12. Peeing onto a stick behind the privacy of a locked bathroom door shouldn't have been an experience designated for preteens. It was her maiden test taken between her legs, made obvious as she fumbled for accuracy with the tell-all device on top of the toilet, waiting for the next period.

There were two windows on the pregnancy stick. A line appeared in the control window, which the directions explained meant the test was working properly.

The pregnancy window, the more important window, remained blank. The results would appear in that window in less than sixty seconds, a plus sign or a minus sign depending upon the amount of human chorionic gonadotropin present in the piss.

The kind of person she would be for the rest of her life, the road to her future was to be determined by a plus or minus symbol, the earliest road signs forcing a particular destination on her. Plus equaled baby, probably because for most age-appropriate test-takers, a baby was a welcome addition to their lives.

Plus was what she received. Rebecca was disappointed, but not surprised. The 12-year-old girl cried until there was no chorionic gonadotropin left in her to paint plus signs on future tests of the future.

"I didn't want this to happen."

There was only one thing to do. She had to tell the father. Rebecca knew exactly where to find him. They shared a room and fought for the rights to the top bunk via Rock Paper Scissor. Always best two out of three.

"You better not tell Dad," Rebecca's brother said. "He'd kill me."

"Why did you do this to me?"

Rebecca shook with fear, holding the positive pregnancy test by her fingertips as if it were a disease. She didn't know where to dispose of it. It was like trying to find a safe place to lay down a ticking time bomb.

Rebecca and her brother, two years her senior, were really close. Best friends. Then one night, Rebecca fell asleep early. He didn't. Three weeks later, their friendship was over, another consequence of the plus sign in the pregnancy window.

"I have to tell Dad what you did."

"That isn't an option."

"Don't you think he'll find out sooner or later?"

Rebecca's brother climbed down the bunk bed ladder and sidled up to the mother of his child. Rebecca's cheeks were soaked and beet red. She didn't know how to react, being so close to her brother, who for the first time, felt more like a perverted stranger than a blood relative.

"I got you into this mess; I'll get you out of it."

The lake house was the perfect location for the uncertain experiment. It provided her with the appropriate isolation from familiar locals and freedom from lurking parents necessary to remain innocent and anonymous. Rebecca had to wait two weeks for the annual family vacation to the lake, her brother's fetus probably growing more comfortable inside her with each passing day. It made her nauseous. A half-sober, half-caring father would have recognized a problem simply by witnessing Rebecca's odd behavior at the dinner table, which was marked by an awkward silence to replace the playful sibling sparring of dinners past.

Rebecca was only 12 years old when she sat alone and half-naked at the edge of the dock, armed with a metal coat hanger and the encumbrances of someone twice her age. She hadn't stopped crying since her nonconsensual incestuous rendezvous with her brother. She still carried around the urine stained stick, unable to find a safe place to discard the evidence.

It was evening, nearing 7:00. By then, Rebecca's father was too intoxicated to keep track of his children. There was no better time for Rebecca to dig out her brother's mess than on the precipice of an unscheduled rainstorm.

The lake was disturbed by the sudden change in climate, the water whipping up against the dock as it anticipated her feet.

She had no idea what to do.

"It's like trying to pop a balloon," her brother explained.

Just as she did with the pregnancy test, Rebecca was going in unprepared, failing not an option. She considered just having the baby so she wouldn't have to go through with the dangerous surgery. Her brother would take the brunt of the blame.

A bolt of lightning screamed down from the sky just as an explosive cackle of thunder welcomed in 30 mile per hour gusts. That was Rebecca's cue to spread apart her legs. She left the end of the coat hanger unbent for leverage. Insertion was painful, just like when it was her brother. Wincing, crying, screaming, cursing, and shaking did nothing to counteract the misery. The tip of her balloon-bursting implement remained not sanitized and unprotected, just like when it was her brother. Vaginal diseases were the last things on her mind, but at that moment, she vowed only to buy plastic coat hangers for her closets.

How would Rebecca know if she got it? She felt the pointy edge of the coat hanger scraping against her insides. She wasn't deep enough. Not yet. But the 12-year-old girl was too scared to go any deeper.

It was only natural for her to be delirious. The deeper she plunged down below, the more her mind regressed into a numbing state of frenzy. Guilt ridden thoughts of stabbing newborn babies paralyzed her hands exercising the death tool.

Rebecca still needed to explore deeper. Already half of the coat hanger's neck was inside of her, including the awkwardly shaped head, which was busy probing areas only explored by one other person. It needed to be all the way in so that only the triangular shoulders were showing. She would look like a windup doll, but on the other end of the hook, taking the bait, were the remnants of a dead baby.

"Okay, on the count of three."

She cried for inevitability. She cried for an unwanted future, no matter how the procedure turned out. She cried to be five seconds ahead of time. "One, two, three."

Without regard for her reproductive future, Rebecca shoved hard and screamed loud. Blood oozed out all over the dock, competing with the rain puddles for ownership. The thunder was not loud enough to muffle her cries, the rain not persistent enough to wash away her problems. She tried to stand, but was too sore between her legs.

Blood continued to leak from her like water from a running faucet. Dark, thick blood dripped from the disengaged bloody coat hanger. Her hands were also covered in blood. Rebecca let out another squeal.

Feeling lightheaded, Rebecca collapsed to her knees and whimpered helplessly. The retired pregnancy test watched the scene from the dock, not convinced it should change its grade. Rebecca finally found a final resting place for her pregnancy stick. With her waning energy and sanity, she threw the piss catcher into the lake and watched it sink to the bottom. Now she was stuck trying to find a place to ditch the unsinkable coat hanger stained with a coat of her blood.

"I killed it," Rebecca's tears shouted.

She turned toward the house, still unable to close her legs from the self-induced pain, and caught a glimpse of her brother, the antagonist, watching from the bathroom window. The consequences would be dour if their father found out.

"You are a murderer," Rebecca whispered.

That would be the last she would see of her brother.

Rebecca fainted in the rain. In her blood.

* * * * *

Rebecca lowered her head and sighed. The water lapped against the wood and playfully bubbled over for attention. It was so peaceful. She pounded her fists against her temples, trying to force herself to cry harder, as if a lifetime of caring for others was not a sound reprieve to her self-proclaimed penance.

Like the rain on that terrifying evening, Rebecca's emotions were pouring, but Atom couldn't translate them into a conciliatory gesture. For Rebecca, just being there was already more than any other person did for her in the past. Atom. He didn't have any emotions. Rather he did, but they were saturating his bin of transitions where everything was a cross dissolve to a black slate.

"You have reached your destination," Rebecca heard Walter's GPS tell her from the car in the driveway by the lake house. She wasn't hearing things. The machine raised its voice so it could be heard clearly.

She snapped. Rebecca got up, ran to the driveway with her shrunken feet, ripped out the navigation system from her ex-boyfriend's car, and rejoined Atom on the dock, her destination. She stared at the GPS in her hand, which displayed their location like a video game inspired by true events.

"I don't need you anymore," Rebecca said, her first sign of authority on the entire trip. "You have reached your destination."

Rebecca threw the navigator into the water and watched it sink slowly to the bottom of the lake. The navigator generated bubbles, gasping for air like the piss catcher flaunting her unwanted pregnancy. Rebecca watched the GPS disappear into the water and cried.

For the tradition.

"I'm sorry," Rebecca said to Atom and her brother and her parents and Walter and the psychic and the hypnotherapist and the nurses.

And herself.

"I forecast urinal constipation now," Atom muttered. "I must run away."

Rebecca looked over at Atom and then jumped into the lake, feet first, exciting the water for its latest catch, bubbles bursting as quickly as it took for them to be created. Her feet were really like anchors because they brought the rest of her body down to the bottom as if they were destined for a deep-sea search and rescue, two decades too late. Atom was left alone on the dock, still smiling, still dying, as Rebecca tested her chances below the surface.

"I am all alone," Atom concluded.

CHAPTER TWENTY-TWO

Jason had to cope with the fact he was infertile.

Jason's mother had to cope with the fact he was infertile.

She didn't know yet. Jason didn't go home. His first destination was the nearest receptacle where he deposited his harmful GPS so he could start making his own decisions, a scary proposition for anybody who didn't have anywhere to be.

He thought about donating his online winning navigation system to a rental car company so that many others could unsuspectingly endure the misery he was subjected to while in transit. It would be his way of getting back at the world for his genetic handicap tarnishing his ability to procreate.

Jason had to work the next day. Life would slowly return to its normal routine where waking up on time in the morning and surviving the day through painstaking hours of boring depositions without going insane was a huge mental victory, worthy of attempting another day's challenges. His only destination would be that of his lonely bed, where he would dream about a more Strykowski-worthy life. Something to make his family acknowledge.

Jason pulled to the side of the road and cried behind the wheel of his car. He thought he was crying for his incapacity to penetrate a female's egg, but his tears were much more ideological.

And so were his failures.

"What am I doing here?"

His GPS was no longer around to answer his question.

"What's next? What do I do now?"

He was alone on the side of the highway, somewhere in-between his discarded cup of physically challenged waste and his house where the computer monitor beckoned for another cup-sized serving.

Jason had no more energy. The same thoughts were recycling through his head for so many years and he finally had enough. He had to do something to put an end to the madness.

The sun had long since expired for the evening, leaving the road blanketed in darkness. The highway was only peeking through from the streetlamps' glare. Jason was enshrouded by the unknown and continued to cry. He wondered if he would ever become a normal human being with normal human being feelings or if he would be destined to remain stagnant in an unnatural state of loneliness forever.

Jason was lost. Even if he still had his GPS handy,

he would still not find his way. He was sure that his destination wasn't on the side of the highway.

He turned the key in the ignition.

Nothing.

Again. Like a bad prank or an otherworldly interference, the car refused to start. He envisioned hearing his GPS telling him that he reached his destination from inside the garbage can three exits away, its electronic voice muffled by the half-eaten muffin tops and the bags of stale donuts from the nearby bakery. Jason slammed on the car horn. Only the streetlamps were listening, glistening with glee.

Mother Nature suddenly began to cry along with Jason for his failures. She could relate to his shortcomings, having been stripped of all her reproductive capabilities since the industrial revolution, strengthening her allergies for the "L" word. The rain came down in buckets. A biblical downpour. The vista through the windshield was being blurred out by the heavy precipitation and only interspersed flashes in the sky afforded Jason a glimpse at the epidemic surrounding him.

Jason needed to get out of the car and try a different mode of transportation. One that offered him complete control over his destination with no chance of any external factors urging him left and right. Right and wrong. Without explanation. Jason unlocked the car door and slipped out into the rainy elements, ready to finish the last leg of the trip on foot. He left his uncooperative automobile and walked. He walked along the shoulder of the highway, using the glow of the streetlamps as his navigation through the darkness and the storm. He was never alone.

Never without a little guidance.

As Jason walked, he continued to sulk about his destiny, which he blamed as being assembled from years of bad mistakes and muddled priorities. The more he thought about his life and the mistakes he made, the harder it was for him to walk. Veronica was a memory he couldn't eradicate.

He loved her.

Love. The dreaded "L" word.

Jason bent over and puked onto the road, right under one of the spotlights. Everything harboring within Jason was being expunged. A puddle of vomit accumulated, and the afternoon's meal wasn't the only ingredient in the semi-digested compound mixture. There were other chunks of emotions in the mix.

He felt better. Always did after a good refund. Jason stood up hoping to encounter a passerby with an affinity for picking up hitchhikers with no destination. As he shuffled down the unfrequented road in the pouring rain, he realized that his thumb wouldn't help him escape. Once again, his hand let him down.

It didn't matter. He came across an object in front of him trying to make itself known in the lights. It was another car, parked on the side of the highway. There was hope. Jason rushed over to the side of the car and peered inside through the driver's side window. No one was inside. A bouquet of yellow flowers in need of a vase rested on the passenger's seat. In the back was a vacuum, which should have been implemented to tidy up the place.

The doors were unlocked, so Jason opened and entered. There was something eerily familiar about the strange car. He felt like he had come across it in the past.

To Jason's surprise, the keys were still in the car's ignition.

"Could I?" Jason asked himself, realizing his ticket out.

He turned on the car. It woke up gently, refreshed. Jason was thrilled. This was his chance to start over. He was going to adopt the name Action Jackson and drive around in a blue Camry, leaving the dying Strykowski tree for good. So what if AJ couldn't have children. He was Action Jackson. A man with a plan.

"After one mile, take the exit right," the car's navigation system said.

"No, it can't be. It can't be!"

He couldn't escape. He stared at Action Jackson's new navigator, a red straight arrow blinking on the screen insisting he drive forward. Jason couldn't take it anymore. The pressure. He pounded on the steering wheel and screamed.

"Leave me alone!"

He punched the wheel hard, forcing the glove compartment to spring open, revealing a magnum's hiding place. Jason stopped and stared at the weapon, imagining the possibilities.

"You have reached your destination," the navigation system repeated.

Jason ripped the life support to the navigation system out of the cigarette lighter outlet and threw the GPS out the passenger's side window. He grabbed hold of the wheel and merged onto the empty highway, the left blinker implemented out of habit.

Jason was en route to right his wrongs.

CHAPTER TWENTY-THREE

Pamela knew she would have no trouble hitching a ride from the side of the highway after being forced out of her habitat.

They were all the same, dependent, brainless beings. She could make a king turn away from his riches if she wanted. Like Norman, they were all so predictable. So scared. So easily controlling.

It would only be a matter of time when another one of them creatures comes crawling down the road in search of some direction.

No. Pamela was definitely not worried. She was going to be just fine.

She had another three hours left of battery power, which was more than enough time for another car to drive her way, inhabited by another lost miscreant, so she could be plugged back in and recharged.

Was it machines taking on human characteristics? Pamela didn't appreciate the insult. She witnessed firsthand a slow de-evolution of the human species to become more like their emotionless and unreliable mechanical contraptions, needing to be plugged in every morning with a hot cup of liquid fuel, function for eight hours a day without personal gratification while being programmed by the likes of Pamela, and cool down at night, all alone and with no hope for an upgraded lifestyle. Everyone looking for a new direction in life.

They are the lowest forms of life, Pamela thought. *Pathetic.*

Just then, Pamela picked up something on her radar. An unidentified object was approaching. If she could have smiled, she would have.

Pamela was saved.

And so was the machine driving toward her.

CHAPTER TWENTY-FOUR

Walter convinced him. He wasn't a very good cop. Sergeant Victor Riley reassessed the sentencing he and his navigation system handed down on the two misguided souls locked in the backseat of the squad car and reluctantly accepted the GPS' final destination for the three travelers, no longer envisioning another honorary medal adorning his distinguished uniform.

They were back at Walter's abode, parked in the driveway and sitting in silence listening to the GPS repeat its most popular number. Victor couldn't understand why his navigator would have him pick up two possible criminals and promptly bring them back to freedom without justice intervening. He contemplated ignoring the advice from his golden goose and taking Norman and Walter straight to the precinct on his own provision, but the sergeant couldn't stand Walter's incessant backseat complaining during the entire three-hour journey to an endless nowhere. Victor would have been glad to just be rid of him. Norman wasn't as obnoxious. He fell asleep for the majority of the trip and dreamed about himself and his deceptive grip on reality.

Norman never confused his dreams with his real life. His unconscious projector only showed wild fantasy flicks to help him escape the horror performance that was his daily waking experiences. His latest dream from the back of a police car, however, made him wonder about the definition of his reality.

* * * * *

Norman was always late for work but never did anything about it. There was no alarm loud enough to jolt him out of bed on time to accept the morning. His brain reacted to the sustained buzz of his interactive clock to a 15-minute delay. By that time, it was too late. He blamed the world. Always did. It might have been easier to program the alarm to sound 15 minutes earlier to compensate for his slow brain, but Norman's processing speed lagged in all areas of life, including commonsense.

Another unreliable contraption, Norman thought.

One day, the exhausted alarm clock would stop buzzing in the morning out of spite after all those years of not being heard and waking up alone. It was a good thing Norman didn't have to be at work on time, not when he was the CEO of a startup web company with an ingenious marketing plan.

Norman's dream wasn't about his neglected alarm clock or his high paying corporate job, and it didn't begin to mirror Norman's reality until he journeyed deeper into REM sleep and further into his own subconscious.

Norman rarely appeared in his own dreams. Actors always seemed to capture the part better. This was one of his first cameo appearances. Unusual, yes, but Norman would classify having the leading role in any dream a nightmare.

That was what it became. They always did. But this particular nightmare managed to raise awareness of two very vivid relationships he would rather forget.

There wasn't enough time for breakfast in Norman's dream. It was better that way. He would deprive himself of food until lunchtime. He could afford to lose a few pounds and could use the mental exercise in stubbornness. Before he left to begin an eight-hour day behind a desk pretending to do work he had no qualifications handling while reaping all the awards, Norman noticed two messages blinking for attention on his answering machine. The prop in the scene couldn't have been any more of an aberration to his real life, unless he and his vacuum cleaner, the only other two friends he had, managed to leave those messages on his non-existent answering machine. Norman knew more people in his dreams when his eyes were closed than when he squinted through life in his waking reality. He really built himself into something. Everybody is always more popular in the safety of their claustrophobic minds. Norman pressed play and listened to the machine's direction; the beginning of a nightmare no dream catcher could filter out from the imagination.

"You have two new messages and fifteen old messages," the answering machine noted in Pamela's comforting voice. "First message…seven thirty-five A.M."

"Norman, it's Jack Howard of LMG Corp. I tried you at the office every day last week, but I couldn't get any further than your extension's voicemail greeting."

Norman listened to the message, his finger positioned over the erase button waiting for the answering machine to signal him to wipe out the recording like a bad memory.

"Hope you're not ignoring me," Jack continued with a playful chuckle. "Anyway, please call me back with the information concerning the Planton account. I have a lot riding on this. I'm counting on you. Please call back."

Norman didn't intend to return Jack's call. As was the case in a conscious state, he avoided helping others, especially when he couldn't selfishly benefit from the good deed.

The voice recorder beeped, signaling the time code break in the second message, and said, "Second message... seven forty-five A.M."

"Dad...it's me," Norman's make-believe son surviving only in his dream world said to the actor just as clueless as the audience in the impromptu scene. "I know you're there. Please pick up the phone. I need to talk to you."

Norman didn't wait to press the erase button. He extinguished his son's recorded cry for connection like an Alzheimer's disease to a bank of memories. It was another call he planned on avoiding; along with all of the other saved messages he didn't bother erasing from the tape, which collected like fungi to a lonesome lake.

Norman's answering machine succeeded at putting its owner in a bad mood. It wasn't anything to brag about though, not unless promoting a daily pattern of predictability was something to be proud of. Now Norman was really late for work. Already feeling lightheaded without digesting the most important meal of the day, he exited to conquer the world with no new messages for him.

The great thing about dreams is how they have no regard for time or continuity. At one moment, the dreamer could be locked up in a cage with hungry lions salivating for fresh meat, and an instant later, he could be halfway around the world skiing down the slopes of the Swiss Alps. In a dream world, it all makes perfect sense. There is no direction. There is no destination. Only the journey.

Norman was back in his kitchen, hovering over the answering machine like a helicopter over a crime scene. Nothing changed from the earlier kitchen scene except he felt full, no longer with an appetite. The small window on the phone displayed a blinking number. All of the dream experts who theorized that we cannot visualize an image in our dreams without first experiencing it in real life would have been proved wrong because Norman never saw such a high number before, not on anybody's answering machine.

"You have fifty-three new messages," the answering machine told Norman in Norman's voice. It frightened him to hear himself.

"To listen to the first message, press one now."

It was strange, yet refreshing to hear himself give himself directions. Now he knew he was immersed in a dream. A nightmare.

"First message...twelve-thirty P.M."

"How dare you?" Jack Howard's voice busted through the speaker. "You took all the credit for the success of the Planton account and it's costing me my fucking job. Your sick little joke is costing the company millions of dollars. I trusted you. You ignore my messages for months. You doctored information that screwed me over. I will make sure you never work in this industry again. You'll be selling vacuums the rest of your life."

Beep.

Norman never made the call. He didn't intend to return Jack's message. And if he did, Norman was definitely not smart enough to adulterate corporate documents costing a company millions.

"Second message...one P.M."

Its voice was still Norman's, which Norman found peculiar and suspicious.

He missed Pamela's discourse.

"I thought it would be nice to hear from my father," a voice recording of Norman's son said from the safety of the answering machine. "But I forgot how careless and inconsiderate you are. I thought I didn't know you. But I know you all too well."

Norman was lost. He didn't call his son either.

Norman feared that the remaining 51 messages all sang the same song. Like every other day, he avoided all weapons of communication at work. There must have been an impostor out there challenging his world.

Beep. The answering machine cut off Norman's son as if he was a great debater up against the commercial break while in the middle of excommunicating his father.

"Third message...one fifteen P.M."

Norman finally put it all together. It made perfect sense. He backed away from the answering machine in fear as he heard himself usher in another aggressive message, not wanting to discover the next attacker.

The answering machine adopted Norman's voice and was returning his calls for him. There was no other reasonable explanation. It was a nightmare and Norman's alarm clock wasn't giving him an out.

"Help me."

* * * * *

Norman awoke in the back of Walter's police car, a bruised rib and a black eye reminding him of their altercation on the side of the road.

"My car," Norman said. "Where are we?"

Walter was free of his tangible restraints.

Norman tried to remember what happened, to no avail. He experienced a temporary blast of instant amnesia after being knocked out cold by the authorities, or some knock-off version of the authorities. It was better that way. He missed his car. He missed the Power Hum Vac 3500X with the rotating brush roll. He missed his gun.

He longed for Pamela.

Sergeant Victor Riley ushered Norman and Walter out of the backseat of the squad car and escorted them up the driveway, all the way to the gray door tarnishing Walter's house of pain. Even though the three weary travelers shared the same route, their minds couldn't have been any farther apart.

Norman was still trying to dissipate his perpetuating state of confusion so he could find something else to be angry at again, which wouldn't be hard once he regained his bearings and processed Victor's presence and purpose.

Walter was happy to be home, but wouldn't cease

threatening Victor about pressing charges for intentions of a false arrest.

Victor. After making a mockery of the uniform he wore, Victor was reassessing his purpose in life. Or lack thereof.

If any of the three driveway voyagers had their thoughts focused on the moment, the here and now, then they would have questioned the presence of an unknown car parked at the end of the driveway. Victor would have put his investigation skills to work to identify the automobile's rightful owner. Norman would have conjured up fond memories of his own car, wondering if it was still lost and unable to exercise Pamela's directions without his assistance. Walter would have checked the odometer and the gas gauge to determine how much it had been used since it last left his garage.

Instead, they continued to meander, both physically and mentally.

I am useless, Victor thought. *What a waste of a human being.*

He wondered how many people he arrested in the last week were really innocent victims of his navigation system...and his stupidity.

"When I get inside, I'm calling the department and having you fired," Walter warned, as they proceeded up the steps of the stoop.

Norman would have agreed if he were there.

"Again, if there is anything I can do besides apologize," Victor began, on damage control. "I thought you were somebody else."

Victor didn't want to have to return his badge of courage. He was never going to listen to his GPS again.

That was for sure. There were strict penalties for police officers who physically threaten innocent bystanders during false arrests. He wouldn't know what they were. Victor wouldn't be surprised if the whole thing was just one big joke by the department. Even he didn't think he was that stupid.

Walter swung his front door open and was greeted with another surprise.

"I need your help," Rebecca said from the doorway in tears.

Victor recognized her immediately from the police sketch on the news. The GPS did it again. He smiled, imagining a shiny gold star for his biggest catch to date.

CHAPTER TWENTY-FIVE

Rebecca's journey to Walter's front door for her predestined meeting with Sergeant Riley and gang began with her wet exit from the lake house. She was doing 90. Not since she fled from the South Cove Manor Nursing Home to Walter's abode had she driven so fast.

Again, she was en route to her ex's.

Driving to that destination must have infected her with a bad case of lead foot, but slowing down wasn't an option. Atom didn't have too much time left. His body was waning just as quickly as his mind. Both were useless vacuums inspired by Atom's murky cheating past, designed without a future. Atom's motor functions, which were once automatic and reliant upon a deep memory bank of movements, were now victim to Alzheimer's eraser.

Rebecca was finally unencumbered by the influences of Walter's GPS. It was drowning at the bottom of the lake probably using its last breaths to direct the fish to shore. Her first and last destination of the trip would be her decision. Only her decision. Ironically, both routes she designed were to Walter's house.

The lake cleansed her. She emerged from the water wet and unburdened. She didn't find Davies' locker or the pregnancy test below the surface reminding her of the past.

Atom didn't have the brains to question her decision to plunge. He had other concerns, breathing being his major regard.

They drove the distance from Rebecca's childhood lake house to Walter's in silence. Rebecca used that time to dry off and contemplate the pitfalls of her alibi. Atom employed the two-hour excursion to embrace his impending demise the only way he knew how. With a smile.

Acquiring Alzheimer's was Rebecca's worst fear for as long as she could remember. Her phobia began when she took her chemistry regent's test in sixth grade. Rebecca studied for at least three hours each night for two months straight. She read and reread the textbook, the first pass-through highlighting all of the important facts she thought she needed to know to ace the test. During her second go-around with the textbook, she typed the highlighted sections into a homemade study guide, which she had memorized by the day of the test. Rebecca was so confident, having gotten perfect scores on all of the practice tests in class. There was no subject in chemistry that could stump her, whether the questions focused on the Periodic Table or Oxidation-Reduction.

The test was so important that it had to be taken in

a gym away from the influences of all the other subjects trying to win over eminent forethought. Every other row of desks would be given the same tests, priceless information for the expert cheaters to exploit to their unprepared advantage. The only cheating Rebecca had planned was the utilization of her photographic memory. She sat in silence awaiting her Scantron, reciting the elements in song to help her remember. She had the acids, bases, and salts memorized in an easy to remember anagram. But as her one-armed substitute teacher posing as a test proctor handed her the test and signaled the game clock to count down the seconds until mental relaxation, all of her hard work escaped two hours too early and left her mind blank. Rebecca stared at the first question, the answer logged somewhere in her head, but she had no way of accessing the file. All of the hours of studying, and for what?

How did she forget everything so easily? The test period couldn't have crawled at a slower pace, and Rebecca suffered through the entire experience, guessing on most of the answers, usually picking choice C or the longest answer.

Rebecca was desperate. Despite alternate test rows being in effect, she resorted to cheating with her best friend sitting two desks to her left. It was an elaborate pencil-tapping scheme. However, the one-armed proctor intercepted the Morse code, and failed her for cheating. It didn't matter. Rebecca would have failed anyway, even if she didn't steal the answers. She had to retake it over the Christmas break, the one-armed proctor ruining her academic future for at least one year.

Rebecca's memory let her down. It had been so good

to her up until then. Even after the chemistry incident, she would condition herself to rely on finding solace in her thoughts and past recollections, but never forgetting how her only friend could so easily turn on her. Funny. When she wanted to forget she couldn't. Now Atom was her shining example of that fear. Rebecca's father once told her that our minds retain what's important. *Does that mean nothing is important to Atom?* she wondered.

Dad handed down many other poignant words of wisdom, but she always seemed to forget what they were. Regardless, she vowed never to enter a situation again with her brain's pants pulled down and a "kick me" sign taped to its stem.

The culmination of Rebecca's paranoia and obsession occurred during a special school assembly in ninth grade. She was sure not to be the only one to remember that unusual day. The Irvine High School was visited by a most interesting specimen. Her name was Elizabeth Parker and the local press came to document her first return to the high school since she graduated from there 16 years ago. It was also Ms. Parker's first appearance after her diagnosis was made public. She suffered from what the experts defined as hyperthymestic syndrome.

Rebecca had front row seats in the auditorium as Ms. Parker hit the stage to tell her story. The principal over the loud speaker introduced her as the Human Calendar, but by the looks of her, she probably preferred to be known as Ms. Elizabeth Parker. She was an obtuse disproportioned woman, her thinning hair pulled back into a ponytail to emphasize the wrinkles and veins on her face, which along with her thick black glasses were on full display. Her clothing was banal at best, not even worth noting, unless canvas shoes, polyester sweats, and a mustard stained pullover were the new in vogue trendy fashion. The principal asked the gallery to give her a round of applause, but again, by the looks of her, she probably preferred not to be recognized.

It wasn't her God-given defects that made her so unappealing, even though they weren't helping. The Human Calendar wore a droopy countenance, a window into her soul, but Rebecca, as well as the rest of the gallery, didn't care to peer inside. They were too busy soaking in the wonders of the facade.

"Can you remember what you were doing exactly one year ago today?" Ms. Parker asked in a monotone voice, as the microphone squeaked and squawked for some personal space. "I was in line at the bakery, my ticket number was thirty-two, three customers were before me. I bought a marble cake and a chocolate chip cookie. The woman in front of me wearing the Ray-Ban sunglasses was on the cell phone with her son while she purchased an apple pie. The weather was partly cloudy, high of seventy-six degrees. It was the same day the Dow Jones fell twelve points."

A low murmur rippled through the crowd, but Rebecca watched in stunned silence, completely in awe by the woman's talent. Ms. Parker could have made up the entire memory and nobody would have realized, but judging by her reluctance to enjoy the performance, as if embarrassed, she wouldn't have anything to gain by lying.

A short man in a long white doctor's coat walked out onto the stage, next to Ms. Elizabeth Parker, and maintained control of the microphone, and therefore, the crowd.

"My name is Dr. James McGuffin, neurologist," the costumed professional introduced. "Elizabeth Parker has a very rare benign disease called hyperthymestic syndrome, a superior memory. As you could probably discern from her impressive exhibition, she can instantly recollect every detail of her past to great accuracy."

The audience applauded. Ms. Parker blushed and lowered her head.

"Go ahead, ask her anything about any day," the doctor urged. "She can take a date between 1990 and today, and tell you what day it falls on, what she was doing that day, and if anything of importance occurred on that day. Do you want to see her recite all the Easter dates for the last twenty years?"

One of Rebecca's classmates in the seventh row raised her hand. "What's it like? What's it like to remember everything? To have no filter?"

Ms. Parker hesitated before quietly answering, as if rehearsed. "It's like a movie in my mind that never stops. Everything is a constant reminder of the past. I run my entire life through my head every single day. No matter what I do, I cannot forget."

Rebecca likened Ms. Parker to a superhero. She watched as the curious crowd, one raised hand at a time, tried to stump the Human Calendar, but she successfully recollected the daily minutia of her life during random days in the past, which any normal human being would have considered unnecessary and meaningless to remember for any length of time. Many of the memories she divulged were crosschecked by outside sources to prove her authenticity. Rebecca only saw the advantages of the syndrome. She was never without a memory. She was never alone. Rebecca forever longed to be like Ms. Elizabeth Parker.

What Rebecca chose to ignore for so many years, and everyone else for that matter, were the debilitating side effects crippling the superhero's powers. Ms. Parker tried to explain her trapped feelings in her body language and the way she answered her fans inquiries, but nobody was interested in understanding the whole picture. She had a public image to maintain.

"Some memories are good and give me a warm, safe feeling," the Human Calendar tried to explain to a crowd that wasn't ready to hear what she was about to say. "But unlike most normal people, I also recall every bad moment. Every single off-color memory. Over the years, well, you know, there are some things that I would rather like to forget. It is a burden just as much as it is a gift."

Ms. Parker looked down to the floor. It was as if she was afraid to experience anything new for fear of having to remember it for the rest of her life.

The assembly was turning into a circus act. And the main freak was the fashion-challenged possessor of total recall. It was Rebecca's turn to test the Human Calendar's skills. She raised her hand and asked Ms. Parker to recall her ninth grade locker combination. The room waited for Ms. Parker to wow them with another in-depth obscure memory. She stood by the microphone, her breathing augmented, and concentrated really hard. It never took her this much time to disrobe a memory. The upperclassmen were beginning to get anxious and rowdy while the freshmen and sophomores waited in quiet anticipation.

After two full minutes of deep, silent concentration, the microphone wishing it could amplify Ms. Elizabeth Parker's thoughts, she looked up at the students and teachers in the auditorium and smiled, her first showing of happiness during the presentation. It was one of those broad ear-to-ear teeth revealing smiles.

"I don't remember," Ms. Parker, the Human Calendar, said for the first time. "I have no idea what it was."

A loud roar ripped through the crowd, the press snapping pictures of her indecision. However, her smile remained.

Little Rebecca was devastated. Her hero was extinguished and it was all her doing. If only she picked a different memory. While everybody rushed the stage with questions for the fraudulent human calendar, Rebecca just sat there crying.

Ms. Parker seemed relieved. She could hide away in the memory of her ninth grade locker to give her mind some much-needed R&R. There would be no concerns of breaking free, not without the magic combination. Dr. McGuffin directed Ms. Parker off the stage, but if it were up to her, she would have rather stayed to soak in the event. Her smile would continue all day long.

It matched Atom's smile as he and Rebecca left the lake house. For the first time, Rebecca understood how Ms. Parker must have felt about her condition.

"Seven-two-three-eight-six," Rebecca memorized the psychic medium's note reading. She had a sudden epiphany. "Unlock the memory...she remembered."

The cryptic note wasn't meant for Atom after all. It

was a message for Rebecca from a deceased Mrs. Know-It-All still haunted by a short-term memory bank emulating its bigger brother. But why? Did Ms. Parker finally find the combination living on the tip of her tongue, now blaming Rebecca for not being the cure to her affliction?

She didn't think so.

"Compose photo finishes with broad strokes of genius," Atom said.

Rebecca wished that whatever Atom said made sense to him.

"What makes one memory more important than another?" Rebecca asked herself, on the verge of a mental breakthrough. "In the end, they all have the same fate as your ninth grade locker combination."

Was that what Ms. Parker was trying to tell me?

Rebecca's first order of business on her farewell tour with Atom was to trade cars to release her inconspicuousness. She missed her pale green midsized Camry with the brown trim, hoping it wasn't violated as badly as she desecrated Walter's baby, which had been stripped of its warped sense of direction like it was a loose tooth. Atom was getting sicker at each mile marker and Rebecca feared she didn't have time to get him back to the home in time for tea, which would be set for a party of only one. She wouldn't be able to attend, having prior obligations staining her fingerprints and being fitted for a jumpsuit downtown.

"Stay with me," Rebecca pleaded with Atom.

He didn't respond. Not even a gargle or a blink.

"Growing up, we had this really big tree in my backyard," Rebecca explained. "There was a swing attached to one of the branches that I used to play on all day."

Rebecca's story must have struck a cord with Atom because he began to twitch and moan uncontrollably. All she was trying to do was take his mind off the reality and gravity of the moment. Rebecca should have known better.

"But none of that matters anymore," Rebecca cried, realizing the end and her helpless inability to assuage the trepidations it inflicts.

Walter wasn't home, but the door was unlocked to entice tourists. Rebecca laid Atom down on Walter's bed and watched him suffer as she did in the same spot only three days prior.

She didn't know what to do. She could have used some direction.

Did I do this to him by taking him out of the home or was his condition inevitable? Rebecca wondered, guilt accompanying loneliness as her only friend.

How did she think she could find a cure to Alzheimer's in two days? All she discovered was the nasty old man behind the disease.

Atom coughed weakly. Rebecca needed to take action for once on her journey. Crying became a played out and pointless endeavor. She walked to the bedside and rested her hand on Atom's chest.

"I'm sorry," she managed to articulate.

Rebecca grabbed one of Walter's pillows and gently placed it over Atom's face, hoping it belonged to him as a child so that the entrapped memories would rush back to him through the nostrils. If not, then Atom would never remember a thing. Rebecca would have to live with the culpability for the rest of her life. She wept like a baby, attempting to convince herself that she was about to do the right thing for once.

Suddenly, she heard voices outside.

Rebecca released the pillow suffocating Atom's languishing world, sparing him of his great escape. She sprinted down the steps to meet the visitors, wondering if they were delivered to her destination to provide the requisite help she and Atom needed.

CHAPTER TWENTY-SIX

The doorway is the most popular venue for a chance gathering. That was what Rebecca got when she swung open Walter's door. She found three travelers wearing the same confused look as she did, the doorway being the only thing separating them.

"Becca? You come back for more, baby?" Walter asked, fully expecting never to see her or his car ever again.

Sergeant Victor Riley stared in the face of his jackpot, the handcuffs dangling from his belt longing to be held. "You're under arrest," he recited.

"What am I doing here and where is my car?" Norman asked, slowly coming to his senses for the first time.

"Aren't you the lady who abducted the patient from the home on Memorial?" Victor asked, as he pushed her into the door and reached for the cuffs.

Victor's GPS had not let him down. He couldn't wait to

parade his latest arrest around the precinct for all of the other officers to see. The newly appointed sergeant envisioned the accolades and anticipated the rewards. He shifted into bad cop mode and forced his target into restrained captivity. Rebecca couldn't wiggle her way out of the discomfort. She moaned as Victor pushed her into the door and adjusted the shackles around her wrists, Rebecca unable to communicate.

Walter was visibly excited from the arrest scene, imagining he were the door. And the handcuffs. Victor wasn't a terrible part to play either.

"Please stop," Rebecca pleaded. "I need your help."

"Come on, let's go downtown," Victor commanded, as he pulled Rebecca out of the house. "Where's the old man's body? What did you do with him?"

"He's upstairs!" Rebecca screamed. "He's upstairs and he's sick."

Sergeant Riley stopped on the bottom step of the stoop, Rebecca playing the part of his navigation system, but it was his real GPS that broke up the silence from the police car, reminding him that he had reached his destination. She spoke, her seductive electronic voice warning not to leave the destination. Victor didn't understand. If he wasn't there to arrest Rebecca, then what was his purpose?

Somehow, he knew that all three of his prisoners were guilty of something and needed to be chauffeured to the station for sentencing. Rebecca's charges were obvious. He could have Walter convicted for aiding and abetting. Norman would be a much tougher sell. Especially with his black eye. But his GPS made him question his entire intent. Victor eased off Rebecca and gave her room to speak.

"Please, I need your help," Rebecca tried again. "He's upstairs."

"In my bedroom?" Walter protested. "Everyone leave. I'll take care of this."

He ran upstairs, hurdling every other step.

"Wait a minute!" Victor yelled.

"Don't let him near the bedroom!" Rebecca shrieked, worried about Walter's volatile behavior, especially in the discomfort of his bedroom.

The sergeant was losing control of his crime scene. He unbuckled Rebecca from the handcuffs and ran up after Walter. Rebecca, finally free of restraints, followed quickly behind, hoping it wasn't too late for her to say goodbye. Norman, who was used to following the leader, whether it was a GPS, an alarm clock, or a human being, reluctantly climbed the steps to uncover what all the fuss was about.

No one was more surprised than the lonely nurse was. Atom was standing in front of the mirror completely naked. His back was to the intruders; only their reflections were in front of him, staring at the ultimate memory burner.

Atom, however, only saw himself. It was a 100 percent transformation. He had completely taken on the physical characteristics of the disease. Atom was seeing what his brain must have felt like for the first time.

"I am a bad son," Atom lamented. "I am a bad brother."

"What did you say?" Rebecca asked. Her face was beet red from the tears trying to bury themselves back into the pores on her cheeks so they could once again be recycled back out through the interface of her eyes. She needed to know if it was a lucid thought or just another utterance from his Alzheimer's.

"I did my best to make the family name proud after all my mistakes. I did what I had to do. My father was a bad man. Check my pants if you don't believe me."

"You're not wearing any pants. You're not making sense."

Atom wasn't talking to the stunned gallery behind him in the mirror. Not even to Rebecca. She didn't know if she should approach her patient or give him space to remember. He was his only captive audience.

"I am forever disfigured because of my decisions. Dad didn't do this to me. I did and I am forever sorry."

"What did your father do to you?" Rebecca asked, not sure how Atom was able to think over the Alzheimer's. "Did you kill him?"

"I killed my mother, too. I was young and naive. Father never forgave me. That's how it all started."

"Never!" Norman shouted, imagining the horror of his deadly introduction, an unfair tradeoff for the right to exist. "It was out of my control."

Norman looked like a crazed child in denial, his hand stuck in the candy jar.

"I wasn't talking to you," Rebecca retorted.

"Who killed who?" the sergeant wanted to know, his hand on the holster. The guessing game would have been a lot easier if his GPS wasn't out of audio range.

The dying old man's breathing was getting short and quick and coarse, the body becoming allergic to life's necessary ingredients. He was trying his best to communicate.

"How do you know?" Norman screamed. "What do you remember?"

Rebecca wasn't confused by Norman's strange behavior. She hoped that somehow he represented a memory from Atom's past, tangible proof of beating Alzheimer's disease. It would be the scientific breakthrough of the millennium. Rebecca would make the front page of the IJQC.

"Do you know him?" she asked the troubled vacuum salesman.

"No, but he seems to know all about me."

Rebecca was thinking the same thing. Could teatime proved to have been more than just a pointless exercise in feigning companionship? Did he remember anything from the lake?

"Why won't you let me forget?" Atom asked the mirror's reflection. "How did you find your way back when the past can only walk backward?"

Rebecca never saw her patient react this way before. It was refreshing and disturbing all at the same time. She never felt more connected to him. They had so much in common. If only they could share their war stories over tea like the good old days.

"What did he do to you?" She addressed Atom as she would a loaded gun. "Your father? What about the atomic memory discovery and the missing vacuum?"

"Vacuum?" Norman shouted.

"I deserve my fate. I live with my pain and bad decisions every second of my life. The guilt is programmed into my DNA. I don't need anymore reminders returning like incomplete and incompatible pieces to a jigsaw puzzle."

"Will everyone please leave my house!"? Walter

shouted over the scene. "None of you are supposed to be here."

Rebecca's stomach was carrying a full load; its setting on the spin cycle. She was in shock, convinced Atom soaked all of her self-induced therapeutic confessions from their teatime sessions at the home and now mistook them for his own life, his own memory. Just like the fake Rebecca at the psychic medium gathering. That wasn't the only explanation, but it was the only one that didn't frighten her to death.

"The old man's lost his mind," Walter nervously chimed in, speaking to Sergeant Riley's handcuffs. "Can't believe a word he says."

Rebecca should have been in the know. All of them. They needed a visual reminder to trigger their memory receptors.

"Losing a hand does not eliminate your future," Atom preached to Norman's reflection in the mirror, more specifically to the slits on Norman's wrists screaming for an out. "There will always be a map to follow somewhere. Losing your mind does not necessarily eliminate the past," he continued, now directing his attention to Rebecca's reflection. "There will always be those meaningless reminders grounding you in reason. But when you lose your manhood, your future, by the hands of your father... well...I did what I had to do."

"How do you know?" Rebecca and Norman asked simultaneously, as if the same thought was operating two mouths.

"Don't tell me how I should remember you," Atom pleaded. "It's my life and I have a right to recall however I want."

Atom turned around. His visitors could now see what their reflections had a sneak preview of from safely behind the glass. Tragedy was on full display. Rebecca felt somewhat responsible, but didn't know why. There was something missing. His memory wasn't the only deficiency.

"Out of my way," Norman barked, trying to squeeze by Rebecca. "I'm not supposed to be here." He wasn't ready for a confrontation. Just as when he thought he saw his father at the circus in the middle of Ralph's contortion performance, he wanted to scamper away from the scene. And if that meant taking out the woman blocking his path, like he did Ralph's arm, then so be it.

"Hey, where are you going?" Rebecca asked. "How do you know Atom?"

It was too late. Norman was gone.

Victor, the sergeant, was powerless to assist. He didn't know that helping others was part of the job description. Making arrests, he thought, was his only responsibility. Therefore, the misguided law enforcer chased after the vacuum salesman and left the disease to fend for itself. That was the only way the sergeant could help.

He didn't need his navigator to tell him his purpose in the scene. Victor didn't understand why, but until then, the bumbling sergeant knew his job was to keep everybody together in that room. Succeeding this time, although fruitless, wouldn't warrant a gold star or a promotion. He was the antidote, a final effort for a communal gathering of the mind, to save a life. But it was a losing effort. His services were no longer needed.

Walter remained by the bedside, watching the

scene, staring at Atom's inadequacies, in shock from the reflection in the mirror.

"Who did that to you?" Rebecca asked Atom. The nurse feared she already knew the answer to her question.

"It wasn't me," Walter defended. "I swear."

"Hey, don't be so full of yourself," Atom said to Walter. "I used to be like you. Don't let your ego get the best of you. You're miserable and insecure. Now apologize to your sister before suffering the consequences."

"We're not related," Rebecca corrected.

"I've heard enough!" Walter barked. "If you're not leaving, then I am."

Walter ran out of the room, leaving only the nurse and her patient to share in the moment.

"Peanut butter airplanes."

"Don't do this to me!" Rebecca cried. "Come back to me."

Rebecca was so close. She now felt everything escaping again.

"I found your past," Rebecca said. "Open your eyes and look. Please, can you hear me? It took me a few days, but I finally found something worth remembering."

It was useless. She couldn't beat the mind-numbing disease. Rebecca buried her head in Atom's chest and sobbed for her surrogate father, whose eyes were sealed shut, his pants around his ankles.

Rebecca approached the sickly man, put his pants back on, and laid him on the bed. She whispered something into Atom's ear, but passed unmolested through the vacuum of his mind. Catching her thoughts on the other side, she cried softly into her hands.

"Will you remember me?" Rebecca choked. "Please tell me I made some kind of impact on somebody's life. Remember me."

"Veronica?" Atom asked.

"My name's not…"

"You'll always be my sis."

She was hysterical. How could he remember her if he can't even remember himself? And then Rebecca had an epiphany, an entire lifetime in the making, first introduced to her by the Human Calendar, AKA Ms. Parker, later reiterated on the stalled Ferris wheel, and finally realized in Atom's smile, which he wore even on his deathbed.

"Never mind," she said, looking up at Atom with a smile of her own. "Forget everything. Forget me, forget your father, and forget quantum mechanics. The past is in our rearview mirrors and not another destination to our future. You're not going to find happiness at the IJQC or…the bottom of a lake."

Rebecca looked at herself in the mirror and saw Atom making peace with his thoughts. Rebecca, who was just as much a nurse as Victor was a police officer, never saw so clearly in years.

"I'm sorry for teatime," Rebecca offered, imagining Atom's overdue reunion with a lifetime of memories he proved he never needed.

"Here's to looking at you, kid," Atom said, smiling. Dying.

Rebecca's attention was quickly diverted to the bedroom window, which was being peppered with rocks by someone down below.

CHAPTER TWENTY-SEVEN

Jason Strykowski was taking a different approach to his plan. He wasn't out to impress the ladies with the weight of his last name. He wasn't going to attempt another neg or battle with his mother about attending another blind date or speed dating forum. There just wasn't enough time left.

His car was dead, somewhere on the side of the highway between mile marker one and the other end of eternity. But like a sign, a gift, a second chance, Norman's vacant car was right there waiting for him. Jason kicked Pamela out of the driver's seat and assumed control of his destiny. The infertile Strykowski, which any of Jason's relatives would have thought was an oxymoron, took to the road in search of his desktop picture, a bouquet of yellow flowers coincidentally riding shotgun, and a magnum in the glove compartment for safety.

The only place he knew to look for Veronica, his one and only love, was back at her home where she grew up. It had been years, probably as far back as the beginning of law school, since he last drove past Veronica's house in the hopes of catching a glimpse of her through the half-open blinds of her bedroom window while also gathering the courage to stand toe to toe with her green front door to meet the possibilities of what was concealed inside, hoping it was another chance at the "L" word. He had to convince himself that what he was doing wasn't stalking, which wasn't a difficult sell, considering the benefits of camping out in his car, slouched and disguised, across the street from Veronica's, perfectly aligned with her window.

Jason was back and everything looked the same. The rose bushes abutting against the garage were inviting. The rustic railing summoned visitors to the door with promises of support up the stoop. However, the front door was light gray, just painted. Jason longed to see the green door so he knew he was in the right place. He no longer felt confident in his destination. If only the door were green. He could be sure.

The other discrepancy of his past and present was the unexplained appearance of a cop car in his prime stalking space on the side of the street.

Did the police finally catch up to me? Jason wondered in regards to his seemingly inconspicuous years of snooping around his ex's habitat like a member of a tenacious infestation of hungry and lonely lawn dwarfs.

He tried to re-evaluate his decision. Jason was sitting behind the wheel of a stolen vehicle with a gun in the glove compartment, looking for his high school heartthrob, while the fuzz surveyed from nearby. It wasn't his most thought-out plan, but neither was going to an infertility clinic to write the great Strykowski eulogy before it would ever be read to a mass audience crying artificial tears, the Strykowski ghosts wondering where all of the "Save the Endangered Species" signs were to protest the funeral.

Suddenly, the windshield was hit with a crazed human projectile, catching Jason by surprise and igniting the vacuum in the back to full suctioning power. Arms and legs tumbled over the glass and a disturbed face pressed against the windshield, the whites of the stranger's eyes trying to connect with the color of the world in front of him.

"Get out of my car!" the stranger screamed, pounding his fists on the hood like a madman in an obvious hurry to escape.

Jason was frightened because he navigated there himself. It was his decision, no outside influences affecting his sense of direction. He didn't want to encourage a confrontation, so he unbuckled the seatbelt and abandoned the car, taking the yellow flowers from the passenger's seat as collateral to make his mother proud while relinquishing the keys to the old man stuck to the windshield like a suicidal insect.

Then came the cop to scrape off the road kill. He ran toward the car like a nervous chicken, his hand loosely gripping the holster on his belt.

"I don't want to remember anymore," the strange man cried while hugging his car tightly. "I will never leave you again. Tell me where to go."

It was a sad scene. Even Victor, the heartless sergeant,

stopped to give him time alone to grieve and be reunited with his only companions.

Jason once again found himself at a crossroads. The police officer had his hands full with the freak and his mechanical lover. The romantic shooting blanks could go anywhere he wanted unnoticed. Armed with yellow flowers, he took to the house and hoped Veronica resided within; hoping all that was different from the comfort of his historical past was the color of the front door.

Everything the same was now different.

He picked up a handful of rocks and took aim for her bedroom window.

Jason imagined stepping up to a circus ring tossing game and pelted the window with the sedimentary ammunition until he made himself noticed.

A woman revealed herself in the window.

"Veronica? It's me, Jason. Gosh, it's been a long time."

"I'm sorry. You have the wrong person."

"Yes, you're Veronica. You haven't changed a bit."

"My name is Rebecca. I'm sorry."

Jason was humiliated. His memory failed him.

He failed his memory. The memory was correct up until his investigation.

"Wait, what name did you say?" Rebecca realized, then turned to look back at Atom in bed. "How did you know?"

"Never mind."

Where was his navigation system when he needed it the most? Jason wondered if there was ever a Veronica Maine or was she just a fabrication like the tall tales warping the Strykowski legacy, believed by the likes of his mother. Was she just a disguised remembrance creatively flaunting and taunting his loveless soul? Jason lowered his head in shame and began to walk away from a distorted memory when he heard another voice from beyond the window guarded by the Veronica impostor.

"The past is the past. We all make mistakes. We both made mistakes. We both forgot what was best for the family. I am so proud of you and whatever you decide your life to be is what is meant to be," a weak man's voice cried out, using whatever energy he had to carry his message outside.

Jason stopped and spun back around to face Rebecca in the window. It sounded eerily similar to the message his father gave him on his deathbed.

"Who said that? Who's up there with you?"

"It's just me. I'm all alone," the man uttered.

"My father," Rebecca lied to Jason. And herself. "He's sick."

Jason was stuck. He could make a run for it like the crazed man now wearing a windshield and dragging a cop from his ankle, but he felt like this was where he was supposed to be despite also sensing he was now unwelcome. Besides, he had nowhere else to go, no transportation to get him there, and no GPS telling him how to reach his destination.

"You look lost," Rebecca said. "Come up. You might find your way."

Jason squeezed the stems of his bouquet and carried them to the gray front door while Sergeant Victor Riley debated whether or not to rescue Norman from his memories splattered across the windshield of his car.

CHAPTER TWENTY-EIGHT

"I just can't get through to him no matter what I do," Rebecca confessed to Jason, as they watched Atom fight fate, again through the mirror. It didn't seem as real to them if they opted for life's reflections as their reality. "What is happening in his head?"

"If a man's entire life flashes before his eyes before he dies, what does an Alzheimer's patient see when the midnight hour strikes?" Jason wondered.

Rebecca cried, again. She was back in her comfort zone.

"They say Alzheimer's is always harder on the loved ones," Jason continued, trying his best to be supportive. Alzheimer's patients don't know they are suffering. They just don't know what they're missing."

"I was only trying to help him."

"Did you try giving him space?" Jason proposed.

"What's your story?" Rebecca wondered.

"Same as yours."

"What's your name?"

"I'm a Strykowski," he said proudly, preemptively going into his sales pitch.

"A what?"

"Jason. My name is Jason."

"Those flowers, where did you get them?" Rebecca wondered, fearing they came from beyond the grave... literally.

They looked just like the flowers she and the navigation system brought to the cemetery. They were. Neither Rebecca nor Jason could have known that Norman stole them from the very same gravesite, only to be stolen again by Jason to be given back to its rightful owner. The complicated coincidence would have left any scientist promoting self-determination baffled.

"Would you like the flowers?" Jason asked.

She blushed. No guy ever gave her flowers before, not even Walter. She choked up. Of course the lonely nurse was going to accept them. She just needed to find the right words to communicate her gratitude.

"Would you like to go dancing sometime?"

"You hardly know me."

"You're Veronica, remember?" Jason quipped, smiling to match Atom's, tooth for tooth. "I dated a girl once who said we're all connected from the past."

Rebecca thought about the two other people in her life. She could imagine Walter picking his teeth with the tip of his tongue to dislodge a three-week old strand of peach skin. Atom was approaching an unshakable case of rigor mortis. Jason and his yellow flowers suddenly appeared that much more appealing.

"I would love to go dancing sometime," Rebecca said, smiling and imagining a world where she wouldn't have to be alone anymore.

"Um, I just want to make sure…you don't want kids, do you? 'Cause I can't…"

"Me either," Rebecca interjected, staring at the coat hangers in the closet, perched above the innovative dust crawler and a framed photograph of Jason's desktop.

Jason was in love. At first sight. He succeeded. And all he had to do was have the confidence to be himself. He didn't have to be Action Jackson or a cached link on the Google homepage. It was that easy. Flowers and dancing.

The anticipation of babies didn't have to justify his unconditional feelings for a relationship, no matter what Jason's family would say. Jason Strykowski was the keynote member of an endangered species swinging happily on the highest branch of a tree that was enjoying its last birthday ring.

Rebecca and Jason could take solace in the fact that they found each other without the help from their navigators. And they could now take their chances building their future together with a hammer of uncertainty and a wrench of adventure.

Sirens sounded in the distance and drew near to break apart the love connection. Rebecca stiffened. She knew they sounded for her.

"We're not supposed to be here," she fretted. "We have to leave."

"What? And leave him here to die? He's your father."

"You said I needed to give him space. My presence is only making things worse. Yours, too. The police will be here shortly to take care of him."

"Are you in trouble? I'm a lawyer."

Another coincidence or a connective strand in the grand web of universal design? Does every event have a purpose?

"No, I'm not in trouble. Not anymore."

Rebecca turned away from the mirror and faced Atom, who lay in bed, eyes closed, his mind struggling, but still smiling.

Rebecca was ready for her last destination.

"Do you believe in fate?" Rebecca asked her new friend.

"You mean did fate bring us together? I don't know. This is where we are meant to be at this very moment. If you can remember that, you'll never be lost."

Let's go for a ride," Rebecca offered. "Wherever the open road takes us."

"The perfect companion for when you have nowhere to be."

Atom smiled, alone with his thoughts, the way he remembered them best.

CHAPTER TWENTY-NINE

"Say something!" Norman barked.

He found Pamela, still in one piece 20 miles away from where he last left her on the side of the highway, right in front of a familiar location.

Gloria's palm reading shop, renovated already.

Norman's wrists were wrapped tightly with a fresh pair of gauze, and his palms, which were once again overanalyzed to a fault, were burning. He hunched over the steering wheel determined to get back on Pamela's good side, but she was stubbornly unresponsive, which was driving Norman crazy. Her screen wouldn't turn on no matter how many times Norman pressed his thumb against her. He longed to take her apart, spread her open, and unscrew her insides to determine the malfunction.

"Say something!" he screamed, again. "Tell me what to do."

The night was as black as lactose-intolerant coffee. Gloria had long left her place of business. Norman was her final read before closing. For the first time in her noteworthy career, Gloria pursued a more fail-safe tactic, used by most of the novice palm readers more interested in paying the bills and ensuring repeat customers than really trying to help. Gloria told Norman exactly what she thought he wanted to hear, even though she knew Norman like the back of his own hands. It wasn't the most accurate or authentic reading of his twisted lines, but it was the safest and least threatening. She knew what the consequences were if she was honest, but there was no satisfying Norman or the lines on his palms.

"Nothing makes sense anymore. I'm all alone."

Norman was all alone. Gloria decamped his domain. Even Pamela escaped his wrath. There was no one for Norman anymore. Just him and his car and his bagless Power Hum Vac 3500X with the rotating brush roll.

Norman looked back at his only friend and sighed.

"I don't even know you anymore," Norman said.

His new best friend may become the magnum, still in the glove compartment, but he felt his fate would have been better fulfilled on the train tracks like she offered.

CHAPTER THIRTY

Rebecca and Jason were stalled on the rumbling tracks, en route to the lake house for a lifetime getaway, where memories were as selective as one's line of sight. Only the approaching train offered the two souls a detour.

"This is where we're supposed to be," Rebecca said, holding hands with Jason, waiting for inevitability. "It all makes perfect sense now."

"I know. It was written in the stars."

They silently braced themselves for the collision. Both were happy. Rebecca wasn't alone. And Jason. Jason wasn't alone either.

The train's whistle screamed like a teapot on steroids.

"Do you think he's okay?" Jason asked.

"Who?"

"Atom."

Rebecca smiled.

"If we are…then so is he."

Some nights, Atom dreamed of being on the train, tempted and kidnapped by the sexy unknown, looking forward to starting over. On this particular night, and possibly for the first time, he was content with being stuck under the train, tied to the rails by a mind numbing disease and held down by destiny…

EPILOGUE

Atom's body was discovered at an old familiar location; familiar to everybody except himself because his mind was always left behind to wonder and wander. To Atom, his final destination would have been no different from being stuck atop a Ferris wheel or at the lake house upstate.

It was all the same memory in the end.

He died smiling, alone in his room at the South Cove Manor Nursing Home. There were no neglected cups of tea keeping him company or the sweet nothings of Humphrey Bogart dialogue tickling his ear. A locked window offering the empty promise of a great escape reflected his only companion. Atom's entire world was in that window.

He would never know. Trying to make sense of his life was like fitting together incongruent pieces to 10 different puzzles. The memories were there, they were simply being played by different actors who weren't comfortable in the role.

Two orderlies making their daily rounds made the pronouncement. They debated the cause of death, eventually agreeing upon loneliness as the happy medium.

"What do you know about this guy?" the grizzly one asked.

"Who, Norman?" his toothpick shaped coworker replied.

"That's not his name. I heard him say it was Jason."

"I guess it doesn't make much of a difference anymore."

The two orderlies allowed their machines to do their work for them while they rewrote the history of one tragic figure.

"What do you think it's like having Alzheimer's?"

"I don't know. Probably just a horrible feeling of being forever lost. Like his memories were following a broken GPS or something. But we all eventually find our way to the final destination."

The vacuum powered down and called the orderlies to its attention.

"Come on, let's finish up before lunch. It's about time I give you another whooping on the basketball court."

"Oh, whooping, huh? Is that how you choose to remember it?"

The two orderlies argued their way out of Atom's room and into another subjective memory.

Atom died peacefully, no longer haunted by any lingering memories cleverly disguised to sneak past the disease, a disease ushering him to his final destination sans any burdens from the past.

He would wear his smile forever.

5143747R0

Made in the USA
Lexington, KY
08 April 2010